Restless
DREAMS

Restless
DREAMS
STORIES

KAREN PULLEN

GusGus Press • Bedazzled Ink Publishing
Fairfield, California

978-1-945805-50-9 paperback

Cover Design
by

DESIGNS

GusGus Press
a division of
Bedazzled Ink Publishing Company
Fairfield, California
http://www.bedazzledink.com

For Jacob, Jamie, Amelia, and Chloe, with much love

Acknowledgements

My thanks to the editors of the following publications in which these stories first appeared:

Spinetingler Magazine, "The Years of the Wicked" (Fall, 2007) and "Scritch" (October, 2010)

Fish Tales, The Guppy Anthology (Wildside Press, 2011), "SASE"

Outreach NC, October 2011, "The Fitting Room"

The Mystical Cat (Sky Warrior Press, 2012), "Gone Gone Gone"

Ellery Queen Mystery Magazine, January 2012, "Brea's Tale"

Everyday Fiction, February 2012, "Snow Day"; April 2012, "Lady Tremaine's Rebuttal"; January 2015, "Brown Jersey Cow"

Sixfold (Fall Fiction 2013), "Something to Tell Henry"

bosque, the magazine (December 2013), "Make Me Beautiful"

Carolina Crimes: 19 Tales of Lust, Love, and Longing, Karen Pullen, editor (Wildside Press, 2014), "The Fourth Girl"

Phantasmacore (November 2014), "Have You Seen Her?"

Reed Magazine (May, 2015), "Side Effects"

Murder Under the Oaks, Art Taylor, editor (Down & Out, October, 2015), "#grenadegranny"

Stuck in the Middle, Writing that Holds You in Suspense, David Bell and Molly McCaffrey, eds (Main Street Rag, November 2016), "No Falling Ribbons"

Brea's Tale

WHAT I MISS most is a long soak in a tub. My last bath was in Fran and Cy's double tub, big enough for all six-one of me to submerge up to my chin. With a few drops of freesia bath oil and the hot water on a trickle, all my worries floated away.

Here in prison we girls take group showers under a pitiful stream of lukewarm water. The guard watches us wash. She has a mustache. She's got no excuse for that mustache—hello? Depilatory? Washing myself is unpleasant here. Nothing here is pleasant.

There are ways to escape. Not literally—don't worry, America, you're safe!!! I turn on my side to face the concrete wall and sink into my memories. This morning, before the wake-up bell, I fled back to my final bath in Fran and Cy's huge marble tub. I had twisted the gold taps full around to release a gushing stream and eased in for a good soak. Afterwards, I dried off with a thick white towel and slid into a soft robe but not for long, as Cy peeled it off, of course, as I knew he would, unable to resist my rosy warm skin. We made love to the gentle sound of rain drumming on the tin roof. My memory of that hour drowned out the cell block's yells and buzzing lights until the outer doors clanged cruelly and the mustached guard yelled to hurry it up, get in line for breakfast. She's a four-letter word and it's not n-i-c-e.

The pillow's a challenge. Two inches of stiff foam encased in a plastic bag, smells like sweat. Next time I see the lawyer, I'll ask her to bring me some freesia cologne. We're allowed to have toiletries. A dab of that on each cheek would mask the pillow stink, ease my glide into the past.

THE LAWYER DOESN'T want me telling my tale—she says it could be used against me. I tell her it's not like I'm confessing to a crime I didn't commit. And "used against me?" What worse could they do?

THE LAWYER HAS a weird mouth with hardly any lips, and her hair is a beige scraggly mess that hasn't seen scissors since her senior prom. It drapes over a gray suit that does her no favors—mousy types like her should wear color. She's wound tighter than a Slinky and always in a hurry, just like Mama was. I try not to aggravate her but I can't help it I talk slow, that's the Carolina in me. I wish she'd be more patient.

You may rightly wonder, who am I—a prison inmate—to judge someone's color choices? Well, I know makeup. You should see my scrapbooks from my sash-and-crown days. In lipstick as soon as I could pee in a pot, on the pageant circuit every weekend from the age of teeny-tiny. For shows, I wore it all—fake lashes, gloss, hair extensions. I sniffed so much hair spray in those days I'm still dizzy. During the week Mama and I had our normal life—she cleaned houses and I went to school—but weekends we competed. We'd drive everywhere—Georgia, Virginia, Kentucky—wherever cash was offered.

My talent was banjo, which Mama taught me early on because I lacked a singing voice but my fingers were strong and nimble and I could pick up anything after hearing it a few times. She stuck Earl Scruggs in the boom box and I'd practice copying the chords and pauses and rhythms until people said you couldn't tell the difference between me and Earl. My banjo was portable, a serendipitous plus when Mama's medical bills piled up, a repo man slapped a padlock on our trailer door, and we moved into the car for eight months, washing in the bathroom at Hardee's, stealing cheese and baloney from the grocery, saving every penny for my costumes and entry fees. One benefit of living in your car—hello? No TV! Plenty of one-on-one time with Earl. The day before my tenth birthday, I strummed the Orange Blossom Special to an orgasmic finish and won Little Miss Southeast with a cash prize of $20,000. We took a room at the Red Top Inn. Oh, never will I forget the bliss of that tub soak.

That year I was nine, honey, I could write a book. I missed most of fourth grade.

I blazed through the pageant circuit for two more years, winning enough bucks for a new trailer for me and Mama to live in. Then puberty hit me like a Greyhound bus, peppering my face with zits, larding up my ass, and adding ten vertical inches. For three years I hunched in my room, practiced the guitar, studied the blossoms on my face and brooded over the unfairness of it all.

Mama had a remission, but she worried about my future since I was no longer cute. She saved my life by kicking my fat ass into the gym. By the time I was eighteen, twice-a-day workouts had melted the lard and I won Miss Dill Pickle North Carolina. A very happy moment, when the reigning Miss Dill Pickle slid the crown onto my lacquered updo. I went on to become Miss High Point, the pinnacle of my pageant career, which ended when I was expelled from Miss North Carolina after I yanked out a chunk of Miss Carteret County's highlights. Drew a bit of blood, even. The witch had stolen both pairs of my eyelashes.

MY FATAL FLAW, overreacting. "Eradicate that sucker out of your psyche," the lawyer says, "rip it out like a weed. Or you'll end up in the Hole."

ENOUGH OF MY glorious childhood. The reason I languish in jail, never to bathe in a tub again, is probably a more important question to ponder. There's the short version, and the long version. The long version explains the circumstances. The short version uses ugly words like *murder* and *convicted* and leaves out the fine details that promote understanding. The long version might even make sense if you have the patience to walk in my shoes. I'm hoping it makes sense to me. Some days I'm not so sure.

I WAS ALLOWED to keep my title of Miss High Point, which came with a grant for college. Off I went to Appalachian State to major in social work, all fired up to wipe out poverty and build families, until I encountered Statistics 201 and Dr. Wu, a grim gnome who rolled his cold eyes every time I raised my hand to ask, "Why does a social worker need to know that?" I got hung up on probabilities and failed the mid-term. Imagine yourself answering this question: what's the average wait at the P.O., if there are two windows open but only one line, people come in one every three minutes and the service is four minutes on average? I knew the answer had to be *it depends* because that's how they do it at my P.O., and it confuses the heck out of some people who walk in the door and see one line and two windows. They'll go right up to the window with no line, and then you have a dilemma—do you tell them to go to the back of your line, which makes you look bossy? Or do you let them cut in and waste four more minutes of your life? That situation is a fact of life, and it makes probabilities most unrealistic, in my opinion, but Dr. Wu wouldn't listen and he wouldn't explain what waiting in line at the P.O. has to do with building families. Unfair, and I needed him to say so, but he tried to wriggle out of my grip and screamed very loudly for a tiny Chinese man until the campus police barged in and that was the end of my career as a college student.

THE LAWYER FEELS sorry for me and tries to get me privileges. They won't allow me to have a banjo in my cell, but she's going to ask if I can play at services on Sunday.

MAMA PUSHED ME to answer the nanny agency ad. She was on her final round of chemo and doing poorly. I filled out the application and passed the CPR course but the first few interviews nearly scared me right into fast food. Twin baby girls? I'm too clumsy, I'd drop them. A trio of boys that needed medication and/or a good whipping. A hovering dad who wouldn't let me give his boy a cookie because "We only eat plants."

The next situation sounded perfect by comparison. The father, Cy, was a salesman, always on the road, and Fran, his wife, worked late hours in real estate, so they needed someone to stay with his ten-year-old daughter. They interviewed me at the agency. Fran did all the talking, in a syrupy steel drawl. "To be honest," she said, "I almost didn't want to talk with you, since you'd won pageants. Who needs a beauty queen living in the house? But now that I've met you, I think you'll be fine, as long as you can teach my stepdaughter some manners." Her horsy face had no expression, leaving it up to me to decide whether I'd been insulted. I didn't care, I wanted the job. I'd have my own room, and I could save money for beauty school. Mama could stop worrying and die in peace.

After one glance, Cy didn't look at me but stared out the window. "Fran reads my mind," he told me later. "She would've known what I was thinking."

"What we were both thinking, you mean," I said. Miss Innocence was not one of my titles.

THE NOISE GETS to me. The girls never shut up—talking, fighting, screaming—and the intercom goes all day long. My cell mate changes every couple of months. Right now it's Susie, a toothless heroin addict who's been jailed so many times it's home. At least she's cheerful, not like those always looking for a fight over love or drugs. Or the passive ones, sad until they knot up with rage and cut themselves. I've learned to be glad I don't have kids to worry about.

FROM THE OUTSIDE, Fran and Cy's life looked good, real good compared to mine and Mama's. Their house was an old place with three stories, much nicer than Mama's tin trailer up on cinder blocks. But once I moved in—my room was on the third floor, with ceilings so low I had to duck in the shower—I realized not all was rosy.

Every little thing irritated Fran—an empty glass in the living room, Celeste's jacket on the floor, a cupboard door hanging open. When Cy was at home, she questioned his every minute: who were you talking to? Where did you eat lunch and who with? I called you twice this afternoon, where were you? She managed their money real tight. She even argued over grocery receipts with Angela, the housekeeper, accusing her of buying extra for her relatives who worked at the chicken processing plant.

Angela fixed meals, cleaned house, and sang Mexican pop the livelong day. She'd been Cy's baby nurse, and the sun shone out of his ass. For someone who'd lived in North Carolina for forty years, she didn't speak much English. Celeste had learned Spanish from her, and the two of them chattered away like chipmunks. Talking about me, maybe, but there was nothing I could do about it so I would smile, pretending they were dissing Fran six ways to Sunday.

Celeste never smiled. She kept her lips pressed together to cover up her protruding eyeteeth. She wouldn't have won any pageants.

One thing I'm happy about—I made Cy get her braces. They should be coming off this month, it's been two years.

THIS MORNING THE mustached guard said, "You're really tall," and I answered her, "Really?" smart-ass that I am. In bare feet, I'm six-one, and I stand straight, thanks to Mama's reminders. Ears over shoulders, Brea. Hunching's a sorry look. Wish I had a dollar for every time I heard I was really tall.

"SOME DAYS I just don't care. Let him fuck around," Fran said to me. "He's been snipped, so it's not like he's going to make babies." I didn't like her confiding in me; she thought I was taking sides, only I never would've taken her side. "Thing is, sometimes these women follow him around, get him in trouble."

I almost didn't dare ask. "Why do you . . . ?"

"Cy's real money is in trust and the trustees have all these rules. No alimony till we've been married ten years. Four more years with that surly brat." Her eyes were pretty, clear and gray, but cold like Dr. Wu's.

Celeste *was* a surly brat. You're not my mother, I hate you, Daddy hates you, clean it up yourself, bitch, you married him for his money, ha ha joke's on you. That was when she was speaking to Fran. Usually she ignored Fran, pretending she didn't exist. Cy could have helped make peace but he was on the road a lot. I was supposed to make Celeste treat Fran more respectfully though my heart wasn't in it.

Celeste's hair wasn't particularly clean but there sure was a lot of it, straight and dark as bitter chocolate. She wore it pulled into a pony tail, which is the worst thing you can do to hair because it breaks. I gave her a bottle of my freesia-scented shampoo, and offered to help her in the morning before she went to school. After her shower, she'd get dressed, then call me to comb out the tangles and blow-dry, smooth the strands around my fat brush. I know that for those few months, she had the prettiest hair in fifth grade.

CELESTE WAS GROWING up and out; her pants were high-water and she could hardly zip her jacket. Fran said they couldn't afford a shopping trip.

"What about your mother?" I asked Celeste. "Can you get money from her?"

"My mother is dead." Celeste's face was so sad I didn't ask her about it, just gave her a hug.

I knew my way around thrift shops, so with my own money I took Celeste shopping. Fifty bucks got her a jacket, three pairs of pants, four shirts and two sweaters. "Next time Cy's home, we'll get you some new shoes," I said.

"Don't tell Fran," she said, "hee hee." Her brown eyes crinkled and she smiled, flashing a mouthful of metal. We became buddies. I starting teaching her to play the banjo and she wasn't bad. Somewhere buried deep in YouTube files there's even a video of Celeste and me singing a duet of "Jesus, Take the Wheel," her serious, me stifling a laugh at our off-key warbling.

I'LL SHARE SOME details you might not know about prison life. You spend hours standing in line: for counts, lockup, meals, urine samples. You get a bar of soap and three huge starchy meals for free. That's it. If you want anything else—shampoo, an apple, a TV—you buy it in the store. Prison jobs pay fifty cents a day, if you are fortunate enough to have one. You get used to the smell of sweat and dirt, disinfectant and despair.

CY AND I FELL into a routine, almost, when he was home. In the afternoon, before I picked up Celeste from school, I'd drive to the woods north of town and park, walk down this dirt road that led to somebody's fields, then follow a path a good ways into the long leaf pine forest. Their needles had made the ground into a soft thick cushion. Scarcely breathing, I'd listen to the trees sigh, waiting to hear his feet rustle in the leaves and his gentle gravelly voice call, "Baby, you there?"

I haven't heard his voice since the trial.

IT ENDED SUDDENLY, all at once. I wasn't there when Fran died, even though Angela said I was.

Here is the truth. Cy thought Fran was out for the afternoon, so we were in their bedroom. It was raining hard; gusts of wind banged against the windows and raindrops rattled the metal roof, so we didn't hear Fran's car, or her footsteps on the stairs. She barged in and started beating both of us with her umbrella. Angela came running and it was straight out of a French farce, me and Cy both naked, skipping around the room, trying to avoid the madwoman's umbrella, Angela yelling anxious Spanish curses, flashes of lightning, Fran screaming, "You fucking slut, get out of my house." Thank God Celeste was at school.

I got dressed and packed my things. I wanted to tell Celeste good-bye, but Fran said no, I had to leave so I wrote Celeste a note saying I was sorry I missed her and not to worry, she had a good future. Then I went outside and walked to the corner, to the bus stop shelter. I didn't say good-bye to anyone.

THE GIRLS TELL me their tales when I'm doing their hair. Their tales are different from mine yet almost exactly like mine, boiling down to one of three versions: didn't do it, did it for some knucklehead, was with some knucklehead when he did it. After they tell it they cry for their mamas, for their children, never for any man. Once it's been told, they don't say it again. Not one is proud of her tale. It saddens me to hear them. I fix their hair and we play around with makeup but you can only do so much.

THE LAWYER TRIED to find someone who remembered seeing a very tall girl in a black hoodie waiting in the bus shelter that day, but no one came forward. As it turned out, that particular route didn't run on Mondays, and I waited in the shelter for ages. I saw Fran drive by—she didn't look my way—and then come back with Celeste, who leaned over the seat and waved at me. I was in the shelter an hour later when the ambulance sped past. I was in the shelter when the police came for me. That's the truth, no matter what Angela said under oath.

THE LAWYER SAID there were no grounds for an appeal. Physical evidence and Angela's eyewitness testimony supported the prosecutor's case—that I had plugged my hair dryer into an extension cord and dropped it into the bathtub where Fran lay soaking. The circuits in that old house had no ground fault interrupters, and Fran was electrocuted instantly. My handprints were on the tub, my footprints on the floor, it was my hair dryer and extension cord. I had a history of reacting excessively when things didn't go my way. The lawyer told me to plea not guilty by reason of insanity; she wanted to try a crazy fired-nanny defense, but I told her I just plain didn't kill Fran.

The jury disagreed.

Guilty, murder in the first degree. Sentenced to life without parole.

YOU LEARN TO treasure any change of routine—Sunday services when you can play your music, earning a cosmetology license, a job in the prison beauty parlor. You explain to the guard about depilatory cream and soon she's mustache-free, whispering "breakfast, Brea" instead of barking it. Her name's Emma and she has grandkids already, even though she's only thirty-eight. She likes to sing, she says, and we kick around the idea of a prison band.

You flee less often. You never think ahead. You live day by day.

SIX YEARS INTO my sentence a letter comes, written in a wobbly hand. The signature makes my heart pound.

> *Hola Brea,*
>
> *Not a day goes by that I don't think of you with deep sorrow and great regret. It was a terrible thing I did, to say you killed Fran, when I know you didn't. My days on earth are short and I need to be right with God. I confessed to my priest and he told me to do what was right. So I am willing to say to anyone that you did not kill Fran, that I lied, and may God forgive me.*
>
> *Vaya con Dios,*
> *Angela*

This letter surprises me. When I think about showing it to the lawyer, I get a sick feeling in my gut. I don't know who killed Fran, and I don't care. What bothers me? That they decided to throw me under the bus. Let's say Brea did it! Yeah! Brea did it! That works!

I talk it over with Emma. Emma's a wise woman with a voice like molten gold. (You should hear her sing "Crazy"—you'd think Patsy had risen from the dead.) Emma's seen a lot, she knows how I am. "What do you want?" she says. "Ask for it."

What do I want?

THE LAWYER'S HAD her hair cut in a chin-length bob but otherwise looks the same mousy self in a baggy beige suit. When she reads Angela's letter her cheeks turn pink. "This is great. I'll depose her right away and file an appeal."

You better, before she dies, I think, lacking the energy to be bitter with the lawyer and besides, I have a future now. The most I can summon up is, "You didn't believe me."

"It wasn't my job to believe or not believe, Brea. I wanted what was best for you."

"How long will it take?"

She shrugs. "Much longer than you'd like. Six months at least."

Six months, six days, six hours. Six of anything is better than life without parole.

I think about my release all the time.

IT TOOK ELEVEN months, but one morning I walk out of prison, carrying my banjo and a suitcase, the one I'd packed when I left Cy and Fran's house. I try on the black hoodie and it's snug. Guess I gained weight on prison food.

The lawyer is waiting for me. She hands me a bunch of newspaper clippings, all saying about the same thing: "Innocent Woman Exonerated." Innocent. I like that.

Her black shiny car has new smells and a computer dashboard. But once we're on the road, the car's fast jerky movements terrify me and the flashes of sunlight give me a headache so it's a relief when she pulls into a grocery store parking lot. Inside there are too many choices and I freeze, unable to decide. I tremble as I wander the aisles. Picking up an eggplant, I burst into tears, stunned by all the colors—purple, orange, yellow, red. When the lawyer realizes she's dealing with an idiot overwhelmed by re-entry, she steers me back to the car.

By the time we get to the apartment complex, I've calmed down. We drive through trees, past picnic tables. It's peaceful here, and quiet. A refuge.

The lawyer points past some tennis courts. "Over there's the pool and fitness center." We walk to a door, climb stairs, and she hands me a key. "Here, it's yours."

I insert the key into the lock and the door opens.

The. Door. Opens.

I laugh, wondering how long it will take to get used to unlocking my own door.

"Your rent will be paid and a stipend will be deposited monthly," the lawyer says, handing me a checkbook as she leaves. "The accountants who set it up can't tell you—or me—who it's from."

So someone owes me. True. I don't care who it is. I wander around, opening cupboards and closets. There's a balcony, sunny enough for a tomato plant. A mirror over the fireplace reflects a dark-haired woman with lots of pale freckles and not even a speck of lipstick. No pageant princess, she. I sit down on the bed—a cloud covered with a floating silky quilt.

Through the bathroom door I glimpse a white tub and exhale the breath I've been holding for seven years. I dig around in my suitcase, find my bath oil, and twist off the top. The scent of freesia, like strawberries in a rose garden, fills every crevice of my poor cracked soul. "Free," I say aloud. Free.

Make Me Beautiful

SONYA WAS MORE confident today, her second day as a shampoo tech, because of the dress she wore—a silver shift that she'd bought from a vintage clothing shop on Melrose. Yesterday she'd been underdressed in jeans and a cami. Marigold had spoken to her about her clothes in a quiet way. Still, Sonya had been embarrassed, thinking a client must have said something about her low-class clothes.

Sonya's job was to chat up the clients, assist the stylists, shampoo, and sweep. She loved the salon. Spot lighting, European-style leather chairs, cobalt blue basins, the latest kind that tilted so clients could lie completely flat. Duman's Salon was a universe away from the cramped apartment in East Hollywood that she shared with her overworked mother, a billion brown roaches, and five younger sisters who rummaged through her clothes the minute she left for work. Here was order, light, perfume.

Marigold, the salon manager, wasn't much older than Sonya, maybe twenty-five. She had slithery blonde hair and teeth so perfect and white you yearned for her rare smile. She'd bestowed one on Sonya when she handed her the thirty-five-page policy manual, covering everything from flowers at each station (replace regularly) to showing up high (you're fired). "Wrote it myself," Marigold had said. "This pack of prima donnas won't argue when it's in writing. You read every word, be sweet, and don't take sides. Or any shit. Keep me informed."

This morning, Sonya's first task was to unpack cartons. She was crouched in the supply closet next to the reception desk when she heard Marigold say, "Uh-oh. Here comes Duman's nine o'clock. She's early and he's late. Where the hell is he?"

Duman was the salon owner, the star stylist, the stylist of stars, or near-stars. Sonya had heard about his client list—directors' wives, reality show housewives, B-list celebrities. And since tonight was the Oscars, they'd be lining up for him. She peeked over Marigold's shoulder—breathing in her sweet citrusy smell— at Duman's schedule. He was booked solid, nine till four.

"Omigod, it's Payton Beatty." Marigold ducked under the counter. "You greet her. She tried to have me fired last month. I couldn't pronounce her name. I said Beatty like Warren Beatty? Only it sounds like 'beet. Beety.'" She sat on her heels and grinned up at Sonya.

Payton Beatty looked familiar, maybe a character from *Law and Order* or *CSI*. She had the frozen expression of the frequently Botoxed and white, white skin that must have come from melanin suppression and peels. Her hair was red, thick, and wavy, with a fine stripe of graying brown roots. Except for the gray, Payton could pass for thirty. She wore a clingy black jersey dress and her breasts looked softly real as she pressed against the counter.

"Where is Duman?" Payton's eyes swept the room. "I need that raghead to make me beautiful." Under the counter, Marigold filed her nails.

"He'll be here soon, Ms. Beatty," Sonya said. Beety. She settled Payton in Duman's chair with a magazine and went back to the reception desk. "What's a raghead?" she whispered, leaning down as though she were tying a shoelace.

Marigold looked horrified. "Don't say that! It's because Arabs wear turbans."

Duman didn't wear a turban, but more questions would sound stupid. Sonya hadn't even realized he was Arab. Impressive, that he'd come so far in this business. Her parents were also immigrants—illegals, from Mexico. They had not gone far. Her mother scavenged for jobs, everything from hotel housekeeping to chicken processing, after her greatest accomplishment, giving birth to six US citizens in a decade as though she needed to get them out quickly before she was deported. Her father worked on a ranch; doing what was never clear. He was the most silent man ever born and only came home once a year.

Payton Beatty crooked her finger at Sonya. "Water?"

Sonya brought her a glass of Pellegrino with a lime slice.

"Thanks. Those cheekbones of yours. Indian?"

Sonya wasn't sure she'd heard right. "Pardon?"

"Or Chicano? Same thing really. Only they're usually short. You know, dumpy. And you're not."

Maybe Payton was joking so Sonya half-laughed and decided not to answer. "Are you going to the Awards tonight?"

"Yup. It's daytime lighting, the worst."

"Well, Duman is a master."

"I've been coming to him since dinosaurs walked the earth." Payton's rubbery smile didn't reach her dead eyes. "He makes it shimmer, like red wine with gold flecks. I just hope he'll be quiet. He chatters in that annoying Turkish accent, I don't understand half. I had a rough night. I don't want to hear about his twinkie boyfriend or dog or leaky hot tub. Here, give him this, tell him to be quiet." She handed Sonya a hundred-dollar bill and fingered the silvery fabric of Sonya's dress. "I think I wore this to my senior prom."

Just then Duman came in the door, dressed in all black, his tanned face hidden by wrap-around shades and a two-day stubble. "Hello, darling, see you in five minutes," he said to Payton, walking through the salon and out the back. The women's eyes followed him.

Marigold squinted at Sonya. "See what's going on and bring him back." Sonya, unsure, trailed after.

OUTSIDE, THE WINTER sun fell in slanted stripes. Smells of exhaust smoke and roasting beans from the coffee shop next door filled the air. Marigold had planted a garden, labeled each plant. Peach roses, orange blossoms, scarlet bougainvillea. A table held pots of succulents with fat waxy leaves and funny names: red-spiked golf balls, hen and chicks, string of pearls.

Duman slumped onto a bench, took out a cigarette, tapped it on the table. "I must quit this filthy habit. Tomorrow, perhaps. What's your name, sweetheart?" He had a delicate high-pitched voice.

"Sonya." She flushed, feeling very young in her shiny dress, and handed him the hundred-dollar bill. "The money's from Payton Beatty. She asked for no talking." She tried to apologize with her eyes.

Duman waved his hand in dismissal. "It's an insult, right?" He lit his cigarette, took a slow draw, and exhaled a giant sigh of smoke. "Hardly matters. Today is a very bad day."

"The work, you mean? Clients getting ready for Oscars?"

"My dog died this morning."

"Oh no, I'm sorry." She knew people loved their pets like family, though she'd never had a pet, not even a goldfish.

"She was hit by a car. I found her on Rossmore Ave, barely breathing. Some fucking driver just drove off, left her there to die. The vet said her back was broken and she was paralyzed. He put her down. Now I'm not so sure it was the right thing to do." He looked at Sonya with reddened eyes. "Have you ever seen on TV those paralyzed dogs zipping around with carts under their legs? Cleo could have had a cart too." He sighed deeply. "I miss her already."

"What kind of dog was she?"

"A Jack Russell. A smart little girl dog. She understood everything I said."

"I'm so sorry," Sonya was supposed to get Duman back into the salon, but how could she possibly suggest it? It was his salon. Marigold would understand that lowly shampoo techs didn't issue orders. She sat on a wrought iron chair and waited.

"Cleo wasn't the first dog I lost. I left a dog behind when I left my village. But I think he survived on his own," Duman said. "I hope. There was plenty to eat and he was a smart dog, like Cleo."

She wanted to get his mind off his dog. "Tell me about your village."

"Nothing like here."

Sonya understood the immigrant's plight. Her parents talked of their past with both nostalgia and scorn: wistful when they described the warm security of a neighborhood where children ran house to house, then disgust at drunkenness and garbage in the streets. Of course, being illegal, once they reached LA they never traveled anywhere again. She was curious. "How was it different?"

"A small village on a dirt road, houses built of clay bricks. Animals everywhere—chickens, cows, sheep. We lived in a compound headed by my father's father. The people were very kind and honest. Then Hussein destroyed our village."

Sonya imagined piles of rubble, a wandering goat. "Where did you go? You were a child?"

He croaked a sort of chuckle and put another cigarette into his mouth. "We escaped to Tehran, then went to Kirkuk. I crossed the border into Turkey. Stowed away on a ferry into Greece. Then I went to Germany and then to the US. I almost lost my life, many times. I was fourteen. Twenty-seven years ago." He struck a match, drew hard on the cigarette, and exhaled sharply.

"That sounds very brave. And now you have everything." She gestured toward the salon's door. "A true success story."

"Means nothing."

What could she say to that? They sat in silence for a moment while Duman smoked.

"Payton Beatty is waiting for you." Sonya said it gently, hoping to distract him from his grief.

"Payton Beatty thinks I am a Turk. Sometimes I say Turkey, sometimes Egypt. It doesn't matter. Kurds don't have a country." He looked at her and cocked an eyebrow. His soft brown eyes were bloodshot. "Iraqi."

Sonya nodded. "People are prejudiced. Payton thought I was Indian. You know, native."

"People are idiots." He rubbed his face. "Okay. Even with a broken heart, I must perform magic. You will be the magician's assistant."

Sonya smiled at his kindness. "I'll hold your hat full of rabbits." She followed him back into the salon.

"FANTASTIC," DUMAN SAID, running his fingers through Payton's hair, lifting up the heavy mass, letting it fall, brushing it tangle-free. He began sectioning and weaving, quick and meticulous, dabbing on the bleach, then the lifting tint. Each time he held out his slightly trembling hand, Sonya handed him what he asked for—a foil, bowl and brush, or tail comb. She loved watching him work. Later she'd practice on her sisters' hair, try to copy his tender skill.

He wrapped Payton's head in plastic. "Now we meditate, darling," he said, "only a few minutes." To Marigold, he said, "I'm going to make some calls," and went through the back, out into the garden again. Marigold rolled her eyes.

Sonya shampooed two clients, cleaned her basin, and wandered about the salon to sweep where it was needed. When Duman returned, he checked the color—"Perfect"—and watched while Sonya pulled off the foils and shampooed Payton's hair. Payton lay back, her eyes closed, the fine scars of her surgeries barely visible along her jawline. Sonya toweled her hair, wondering how Duman would style her. Payton had perfect features and could wear any style.

He began by taking off an inch, then layering. He textured the edges to give them a softer line. As he sectioned her bangs, Payton's phone rang and she began a conversation with someone about her date for the Oscars—"gay as a daffodil," her hair— "Duman's making me beautiful," and her exhaustion after only two hours of sleep. "I hit something last night, might have been a dog, from the yelping," she said. "Why do owners let their dogs out? It's so irresponsible." She closed her eyes and listened to her caller. "Too late to stop. I was coming out of Wilshire Country Club. On Rossmore? Just going along with traffic. God, it was horrible. I was shaking for hours. Of all the nights I needed my rest. It took me forever to get to sleep."

Sonya, sweeping under Duman's counter, froze in horror. She looked at him. Had he heard? His face was bluish white, and there was a film of moisture on his upper lip. Would he say something to this stupid, stupid woman? He continued to work. Delicately he took a section of hair, then a roller brush, sliding it to straighten the hair away from her scalp. He turned to Sonya and held out his hand for the hair dryer.

Something should be said. Or done.

Sonya set the broom aside and opened his scissors drawer. She selected a pair and held them out, tentative. Their eyes met. Duman's were intense, full of pain. He took the scissors, and she felt a pulse of glee at his courage and her daring.

With a single snip, he cut the section of hair close to Payton's scalp. He took another handful and stretched it out with the roller brush then severed it with scissors, again at the scalp.

Sonya watched, fascinated. Duman lifted and cut, lifted and cut, his scissors clicking as carefully and quickly as ever. It was horrible. Payton was unaware; her back to the mirror, she chattered into her phone. He was very nearly finished when she looked up. Perhaps she sensed the coolness of her near-baldness, or the weightlessness. She twisted, looked in the mirror and howled, "Oh my God! What have you done to me?"

Her head wore a patchy uneven stubble. A reddish coil hung over her cell phone ear. The bangs had been spared, and the contrast between the nearly-bald scalp and the fringe that fell to her eyes was comical. Duman ran his hand over her stubbly scalp. "Almost done," he said. "What do you think?"

With a shriek Payton twisted out of her chair and slapped him with a hard crack. The sound of it hushed the salon like an off switch, and all eyes turned to Duman and his client. Marigold jumped up and started towards his station.

"Don't." He held up his hand to stop her. "Let's finish it off." He picked up the electric razor. "It would be merciful."

Payton grabbed Sonya's broom and swept everything off his counter—jars, flowers, photographs. "I'll sue, you fucking idiot! What am I supposed to do now?" She wrapped her arms around her head and moaned. The entire salon—stylists, techs, and clients—froze, then someone raised her cell phone and recorded the scene. *Tap, tap, tap* went more phones.

Marigold hurried to shield Payton from the cameras. "We'll make this right. Come with me. Free wig." She gave Duman a push and he stumbled, off balance, stepping backwards. Sonya caught his arm.

THE PHOTOGRAPHS SPLASHED instantly into the twitterverse, then onto *Extra*, *TMZ*, and dozens of celebrity scandal sites. And later, wherever Sonya worked, when they learned she'd been there that day, she had to retell the legend of Duman, Kurdish hero to dog lovers everywhere. But she always left out what happened next.

She'd walked with Duman through the hushed salon, outside to the garden where he wailed like a child, great hiccupping wails. She let him cry, patting him on the back—her sisters were great criers and you just had to let them go at it. Heat rose off him like a radiator.

"I really fucked up, didn't I," he said when he calmed down.

"You are a brave man," Sonya said. "I have only admiration for you."

"She'll probably sue the salon. Americans like to sue."

Sonya moved so she could see into his eyes. "People will sympathize with you. Everyone loves dogs."

"Marigold must be furious."

"Will she fire me?"

"Nah. I'm to blame. She'll just add another rule to her manual." He laughed, the cracked laugh of a man who smoked too much and laughed hardly ever. "Maybe I have created a new style. The refugee buzz."

"All the clients will be asking for it," Sonya said. "No shampooing necessary. I'll be out of a job."

"No, no, we'll style dogs too! Bring your dirty dogs to Duman's!"

Relieved that he was joking, picturing the salon full of half-bald clients and sudsy poodles, Sonya giggled, and her laughter was infectious and made him laugh even more until they were both shrieking. He pounded the table, both of them helpless to stop as tears filled their eyes.

The Fourth Girl

WHEN THE PRINCIPAL told me he wasn't going to renew my contract, I smiled numbly and slouched out of his office, saving the tears of humiliation for my walk to the bus stop. Weeping, cussing, I almost didn't answer my cell phone.

"Reenie Martin?" Speaking in a crusty solemn voice, the man identified himself as a lawyer. "Your Aunt Peggy has passed away. She's left you her entire estate—her house, her car, and liquid assets."

Life *is* fair! The universe *does* care! Visions of stock portfolios, a cottage surrounded by white picket fence, and a life far, far away from the New York City public school system danced through my head. I brushed away the tears of the recently fired and shrieked with glee. Scooping up Mango, my orange tomcat, for a furry hug, I danced around my coffee/dining/desk table, bounced on the daybed that also served as my sofa, then rummaged through my tiny fridge for a beer, the closest I could get to bubbly.

OK, back up. I wasn't ecstatic about Aunt Peggy's death, but not saddened either, as our relationship consisted of a card exchange at Christmas. I lived in Brooklyn, she in North Carolina, and our paths hardly ever crossed. She was my father's much older half-sister. So this windfall, this unexpected bounty, wasn't accompanied by grief. Curiosity, mainly. What kind of life had she lived? What life would I be stepping into?

I was eager to leave New York. A, I couldn't afford to live here. B, nearly all my friends had married, moved to the suburbs, and produced two-point-one kids. C, my most recent romance had ended in a shouting match worthy of the Jerry Springer Show. (Did you know there's a Blackberry app that tells his wife his exact location—not his office on Broadway, where he's supposed to be working late, but a restaurant on West 43rd, where he's eating sushi with me? No? He didn't either.)

I'd come to the conclusion, based on personal experience, that any New York man interested in me was either a cheater or a mouth breather. But getting fired was the straw that broke this thirty-two-year-old's ties to the Big Apple. I shoved my clothes and books into a dozen boxes and called UPS for a pickup. Said *adieu* to my studio apartment, a twelve-by-twelve space with one grimy window overlooking an alley of dumpsters. Slid Mango into his carrier, took the subway to Penn Station, and boarded a train for the twelve-hour trip to Raleigh, dreaming Martha Stewart fantasies of a real house. With a garden. Maybe even chickens. Martha has chickens. And goats. I could make cheese.

"WHY ME?" I asked.

The crusty solemn voice belonged to a spare, white-haired man with a benign expression of lawyerly rectitude. "You were her only living relative, Reenie. She was once an English teacher, like you. She was adamant women should have financial independence."

I'd forgotten Aunt Peggy had been a teacher too. My concept of the size of her "estate" fizzled. "What can you tell me about her?" I could hardly wait to see my new house and let Mango out of his carrier, but this man had known my aunt for years, would know her friends, her life.

He tapped his lips then appeared to choose his words. "A very private person. You'll meet her friends; I'm sure they'll stop by. What are your plans for the house? Going to sell it?"

"I'm going to live in it."

He raised one graying eyebrow. "Indeed. Well then, welcome to Verwood." He handed me a set of keys. "Doors, garage, car. I transferred her bank account to your name. Sign here, please."

I scanned the form, a statement of my newly inherited assets. A house plus 2.3 acres at 601 Wiley Jones Road, a 2005 Toyota Camry, a bank account with a balance of $6,754.52. Not much. I'd have to get a teaching job. I shuddered.

I WASN'T USED to driving, but there was so little traffic in Verwood that I felt no qualms about steering the Camry onto the highway and four miles later onto Wiley Jones Road. I passed three trailers before I saw 601's mailbox and turned onto a washboard driveway winding through vine-covered underbrush and towering pines.

And there was my bungalow, one story with a crumbling front porch, neglected hollies growing up to a rusty tin roof, plywood covering a broken window. And out back, a tiny rough-board shed surrounded by a wire fence—a chicken coop!

I was beyond excited. My Martha instincts kicked in—this house could be *cute*. Mango meowed plaintively in the carrier. "Your ordeal is over. We're home, boy," I said, skipping up the steps.

Oh my. I'd landed in the seventies. Shag carpet so grimy you couldn't tell its original color. Flocked wallpaper. Avocado green sofa and chairs, the upholstery worn down to the foam. A dark room made darker by heavy brocade draperies at the windows. Mango began to explore, tentatively sniffing every square inch of that carpet. I counted seventeen candles burned down to wicks, and any number of dust-covered silk flower arrangements. But I couldn't stop smiling, so happy was I to have my own place. With a fireplace!

And a letter on the mantel, addressed to me:

> *Dear Reenie,*
>
> *It gives me great pleasure to know you will be my beneficiary. I realized many years ago that teachers work very hard for little pay, even less status and no chance of advancement, so I am delighted you can benefit from my experience.*
>
> *Twenty years ago I found another way to make money with little work and no stress, and I hereby bequeath it to you.*
>
> *In addition to my cottage, you have inherited a home-based business that ticks along without much effort. It will generate enough income to pay your*

expenses if you live modestly. Five days a week, my girlfriends Connie, Fran, and Lilac arrive just before noon. Shortly thereafter, three clients appear at your door, one per girl, and each couple disappears into a bedroom. At the end of one hour, each client will hand you $50, tax-free, and depart, smiling. (They pay the girls separately.)

I hope you enjoy living in Verwood as much as I did. People are friendly but fortunately for me and now for you, they mind their own business. No one seems to care about my little lunch-time club, and that's the way my girls and their clients like it.

From this day forward, you'll be able to see a yellow school bus without shuddering.

Much love,

Aunt Peggy

My mouth dropped open: I had inherited a brothel.

My good-girl Methodist side was horrified, but Peggy's clever reminder of yellow-bus-dread hit home, making my pragmatic burned-out side think *What the hell! This could work.*

But what were the girls like?

THE GIRLS SHOWED up at eleven-thirty the next day, a Friday, and what astonished me was how ordinary they looked, like any forty-something women waiting on a Bronx subway platform. Lilac was a petite blond with thick glasses, missing an incisor. Fran wore a long flowery dress that disguised her too-ample curves, while Connie, in purple skinny jeans, had lovely cheekbones and knock-knees. In no time we were chatting about their families, diets that didn't work, best store for shoes. And their clients.

"Each one's different," Fran said. "Some might say peculiar." She giggled, and her whole body rippled. "A regular schedule, the same ones each day of the week."

"We're picky," Lilac said. She was studying a Scrabble word book.

"What's today, Friday? My dentist. He likes to be scolded," Connie said. She'd changed into an eighties-style power suit, red lipstick, and heels. She took out a knitting project in blue yarn, "a sweater for a Siamese, to match its eyes." She told me she knitted clothing for pets and sold it on Etsy. She was saving to send her son to college.

Lilac looked up. "'Siamese,' that's an easy bingo." She explained that she played competitive Scrabble, and a bingo meant a word that used all seven tiles. "My client today is the fire chief. We usually play a game after our feather frolic."

Feather frolic? My mind boggled.

Fran squeezed herself into a naughty nurse uniform "for the professor" and offered me a homemade toffee. Hard at first, the sticky candy melted in my mouth, leaving a hint of chocolate mint. "I sell them at the farmer's market," she said. "If there's any left!" She laughed, severely testing her costume's seams.

As they waited for their clients, they gossiped. Connie bragged that her son made the honor roll, and Fran said she ought to be proud, he was one fine boy. Lilac told a story about her dog humping the plumber who was replacing her garbage disposal. Connie knitted, Lilac studied word lists, and Fran nibbled, until *clonk clonk* went the door knocker. I ducked into the kitchen, to watch from behind the door.

The first client was Fran's professor, a jockey-sized man with a goatee. He hung his tweed jacket in the hall closet and began to limp, whimpering with each step. *What a faker*, I thought.

Fran tugged up her red thigh-high stockings, tucked a stethoscope into her cleavage, stroked his cheek. "How're you doing, sweetheart?"

"I feel terrible, from head to toe, just terrible."

"Let's check you out. Exam room one." Fran sashayed down the hall to the bedrooms, beckoning him with a crooked finger to follow.

Clonk clonk, and the front door opened again. The dentist was a paunchy man with thick white hair, smelling of Old Spice. He planted himself in front of Connie, who didn't even glance up from her knitting but said, "Go to your room. You have been a very bad boy." Looking hang-dog guilty, he slinked down the hall. Connie slid a marker onto the needle and put her knitting away. She took a ruler from the closet and followed him, smacking the ruler against her palm and growling for him to hurry.

Lilac pushed aside the heavy brocade draperies, looked out the window. "Chief is always last." She poked inside a tote bag. "We could use some new feathers. Chief took a few home last week."

OMG. I closed the door. I'd seen enough. I spread a drop cloth over the kitchen floor. I'd decided to paint the burnt orange kitchen's walls and ceiling a creamy ivory. As I spackled and taped, I worried. Last night's heavy rain had proved too much for the rusted roof, and I'd dashed around putting pots under a half-dozen leaks. Clearly I needed a new roof. As far as beautification went, I'd whacked the hollies into submission. But my Martha-vision included paint, landscaping, better furniture, repairing the front door, replacing heavy draperies with white sheers, grading the quarter-mile driveway, and a lot of fencing (for the goats I didn't yet have). Obviously I needed more income. I'd ask the girls what I should do.

"DON'T RAISE YOUR prices," Lilac said. "Once Peggy went up twenty bucks and we lost a bunch of guys."

"What about taking on a few more clients?" I asked.

Connie frowned. "You mean two in one day?" They exchanged looks. "That's like cheating."

"Yeah. Each client has his day, no sharing," Fran said. "Like a date."

Whatever. "Alrighty then," I said, "we need a fourth girl." I studied the three women. Connie's face was getting that crepey look. *She's experienced, surely that's desirable?* Fran's belly bulged; you could see her red thong where her zipper had come unstitched. *Oh dear.* And Lilac—squinting at her word book—she should replace that missing tooth. *Not a good look.*

Funny, the regulars didn't seem to mind.

"It shouldn't be hard to find one," Lilac said. "The economy and all."

"I don't know where to look," I said.

Connie said, "Try Walmart. Or Target."

I imagined wandering around discount stores for hours, the horrified expressions of sales clerks and customers as they realized the job I was offering. "I don't think so," I said.

"I could check out the lady farmers at the market," Fran said. "They could use the cash but they're a bit weathered, if you know what I mean."

Lilac looked up from a list of words containing Z. "What about Splits and Tits?"

"What's that?" I asked.

"Strip club. Girls gyrating around poles. Neon lighting kept dark so customers can't see cellulite and varicose veins."

"Lilac, you're a genius. Sounds perfect."

I made up business cards with an image of hundred-dollar bills raining down. *Part-time work, easy money!* I drove to Splits' parking lot and as the dancers arrived for work, I handed out my card. "Call me," I say, waggling my thumb and pinky. "Guaranteed income, homey surroundings."

BY THE FOLLOWING Friday I had my fourth girl.

A redhead with a cockney accent, Ginger wobbled slightly on five-inch leopard-skin heels. She wore a black leather teddy decorated with fishnet and straps and nailhead trim. She sauntered into my living room and looked around. "Place seen better days, innit?"

Lilac's eyes widened, but she offered a friendly "Hi." Fran held out her box of toffee, and Connie said, "It's great to have a new face here."

Impressed they were so welcoming, I told them my plan. "I'll introduce Ginger to your clients, and ask them to spread the word."

"Why not let her take our place today?" Connie asked. "We talked about it, and we three could use a day off." Fran and Lilac nodded.

"Will your clients object? They're awfully fond of you," I said. "Used to a certain, uh, routine."

Connie shrugged. "Tell them we'll be back next Friday." She gathered up her knitting. Lilac said she'd find an online Scrabble game. Fran wrestled off the naughty nurse costume and pulled on stretchy waist jeans and a tee shirt. They left, seeming pleased to have free time.

ONE BY ONE, the regular clients arrived. I ushered the professor into the bedroom where Ginger waited, dressed in the naughty nurse costume taken in with safety pins. She wriggled seductively as she beckoned him to lie down. "Let's take a look at you, dearie," she said, twirling the stethoscope.

The professor frowned. "Uh, you're a skinny little thing, aren't you? Except for those basketballs on your chest."

I closed the door. Surely Ginger could work through his crankiness. She'd assured me she knew how to make a man happy.

Five minutes later, he stormed into the living room, shoving his money at me. "It better be Fran next week, right?" He stomped out.

I knocked on the closed bedroom door. "You OK?"

"Hell yeah. Daft old sod."

When the dentist arrived, Ginger had changed into a tweed suit with big shoulder pads. She ordered him to sit on a stool in a corner, facing the wall. She started scolding him, as Connie would have, and I left, thinking *this one will be OK*. But soon, too soon, from the bedroom the dentist yelled, "That's not right! You're doing it all wrong!" He left, weeping, refusing to pay.

I sighed. Transitions are rough.

Ginger came out, dressed in her leather teddy. She rolled her eyes. "What a perv. OK, bag of feathers?" She tucked the Scrabble board under one arm, gathered a bouquet of feathers, and waited by the window for the chief, who was late as usual. "Firefighters are buffed, aren't they? Hang around the station doing press-ups? I'm ready for a real man." A moment of silence, then, "What's this? Looks like a social worker."

I put down my paint roller and glanced out the window at a woman with short dark hair, big sunglasses and a navy pantsuit, admiring my bed of annuals. She clacked the door knocker.

"Is Lilac here?" the woman asked, when I opened the door.

Lilac hadn't mentioned that the fire chief was a woman.

"Bugger all." Ginger dropped the bouquet of feathers and the Scrabble board. "I don't roll that way. What kind of place is this? Where's a normal man?"

I had to think a moment. "Define 'normal.'" I sent the chief away, whispering that Lilac would be back next week.

What a huge mistake I'd made. "Ginger," I said gently, "it's not working. My clients are used to my girls. They don't want anyone else."

Ginger hissed, "You're making big lolly here off twats and lezzies and I want five thousand dollars to keep my piehole shut. Or else I tell the coppers."

"What?" I needed that money for a roof, siding repair, furniture, a fence. "Give me a week, honey. I'll see what I can do." I gave Ginger a little push out the door, gratified to see her lose her balance and nearly fall off her fuck-me shoes.

THE FOLLOWING FRIDAY, noontime, the girls waited for their regulars. Connie was knitting doggie booties out of gray heathery yarn, a complicated pattern with double-pointed needles. Fran offered me a piece of toffee topped with chocolate and almonds. *So* so good, but quite a jaw workout to dissolve it. Lilac was absorbed in a word list, muttering what sounded like *drachms, klatsch, scarphs, schmalz, schnaps, sclaffs, scratch*.

I told them Ginger would be along soon. "She wants severance pay to keep our little business a secret. So I'm off to the bank, to withdraw funds. When she shows up, ask her to wait."

The girls exchanged looks. "Don't worry, Reenie," Connie said. "We'll manage."

A HALF HOUR later, back from the bank, I parked the Camry in the garage and entered my house through the laundry room. I passed the bedrooms, briefly listening at each door. I heard Connie barking orders, Fran's directive to "Say 'Ah,' baby. . ." and the chief's feather-induced giggles. All was back to normal, or near-normal, except for Ginger's threat. I was thankful the girls forgave my mistake, relieved the clients came back. Now I only had to negotiate a more modest payment to Ginger.

But Ginger wasn't waiting impatiently for her blackmail money.

She lay face down on the living room floor, her stiletto-clad feet splayed wide in a scatter of toffee candies and Scrabble tiles. She clutched to her neck a tangle of gray heathery yarn and double-pointed knitting needles. One of the needles had punctured her throat, and blood oozed from the wound into the shag carpet. My heart ratcheted into overdrive as I knelt and searched for a pulse. None. Ginger was surely dead, the body still so warm that Mango had wedged himself against her hip.

I pounded on the bedroom doors. "Get out here! Now!" As soon as the girls and their clients emerged, I questioned them. "What the hell happened?"

Fran clasped the professor to her bosom. "We didn't hear anything," she said.

"Me either." Lilac looked frightened, and the chief patted her back.

All six denied hearing or seeing Ginger. "She must have come in while we were in the bedrooms," Connie said. "Was it a break-in? Anything missing?"

My mind reeled as the girls, the clients, and I stared at each other in shock and mistrust. A burglary gone wrong? Had one of the girls killed her out of spite? Or to save me from blackmail? Or maybe one of the clients killed her, in the mistaken belief that Ginger was going to replace his favorite. Irrational motives, bizarre means. Alibis all around—or were they?

I called the police.

"LOOKS SUSPICIOUS, ALL right," said the detective, solidly built in a snugly fitting tailored uniform, a sight that normally activated my flirt gene, but today I was angry at the official attention and very very worried. First and foremost, what happened to Ginger, in my house? Was this death going to destroy my brand-new business, drive my girls onto welfare rolls, disgrace my clients?

A forensic team booted us out. The three girls, their Friday clients, and I went to the police station to be interviewed separately, but we all had alibis and the clients were solid citizens. The detective brushed off the issue of three couples in my bedrooms.

"I'm investigating a death, not misdemeanors," he said. "Everyone knew your aunt ran a lunchtime social club. No harm done."

Whew. One less thing to worry about, and I mentally smacked my forehead—Ginger's threat to tell the police had been empty.

After a few hours, they allowed us to return. Connie was annoyed because they'd confiscated her needles and yarn. Since they'd also gathered up the Scrabble tiles, Lilac would have to buy a new set. Fran shrugged; she could always make another batch of toffee. We gave each other hugs, and they departed, leaving me alone in a house with a blood-stained shag carpet.

I checked the locks on my doors and windows. It would be a long time before I could forget the picture of Ginger's still body, posed as though she'd collapsed without a struggle, a size four double-pointed knitting needle piercing her throat. I'll admit it—I was afraid. To distract myself from my fears, I began to spray the flocked wallpaper with water and peel it off the wall. Mango watched me work, the tip of his tail twitching. *What did you see, Mango?*

"IT WASN'T MURDER," the detective declared, a statement I had trouble believing until he explained. "Forensics worked this case over good. Ginger's fingerprints covered Connie's on that needle, meaning no one else held it. And the ME found a big wad of toffee lodged in her throat, and cat hair on the toes of her shoes. So here's a likely scenario. She was annoyed with you all, right?"

I nodded. "I'd promised her employment, but it didn't work out."

He nodded and smiled, a crooked smile showing white teeth, a nice contrast to his warm brown eyes. "She knocked the Scrabble tiles to the floor and stuffed three toffees in her mouth.

Those toffees don't dissolve easily; they turned into a sticky mass, making it difficult to swallow. She grabbed the knitting project, intending to pull it apart, but as she began to choke, she clutched her throat, tripped over the cat in those ridiculous shoes, slipped on the tiles, and fell onto one of the needles. She stabbed herself. Case closed."

Sweet words. *Case closed.* I thought they only said that on TV.

WE WERE ALL *so* grateful to the detective, whose name was Jack. Fran gave him a tin of assorted toffee, Connie knitted a stylish black sweater for his bulldog, and Lilac—well, she offered a feather frolic that he gracefully declined, claiming an allergy.

One night, I cooked him dinner, and he was so appreciative that he came back the next morning with tools. Together we ripped up the bloodstained carpeting. A filthy job made tolerable by the way his shoulders moved under his tee shirt.

I offered Jack a beer. "We're a sight," I said. Visible grime coated his face and arms.

He tipped the can for a swallow, then another. "A shower would be nice."

"Use mine, if you like," I said, glad that I'd put out clean towels that morning.

"Ladies first," Jack said. "Or, might I join you? You know, for lunch?"

And just like that, I realized that the fourth girl had been here all along.

No Falling Ribbons

THE WALLS ARE so thin Michael says he hears the neighbor fart, but I sleep through anything—yells in the hallway, TV next door, motorcycle revups in the parking lot. But this morning, the soft click of a closing door nudges me awake. Michael's gone out.

It's still dark, too early to get up. In an hour the light of day will wake the baby so I try to go back to sleep. I count my breaths and picture a flat sandy desert but fears about Michael whine about like mosquitoes and keep me awake. A headache starts up, an old familiar headache, no friend to me.

I don't want to worry but can't help it. Has he gone to work? Will he be on time and last the day? His job starts at seven so he should make it, he's left early enough, though he'll stop to get high because he can't work sick. It's his first real job in months, on the janitor crew at Holy Family Hospital in Methuen. It's a good job, with benefits. My unfabulous job, waiting tables at Jerry's Barbeque, has no benefits unless you count the free meal I always skip—I could puke just thinking about the grease. And these are only the everyday fears. Over them all, like a damp cloud of radioactive dust, hovers the nightmare of Michael curled up in a drain pipe, dead of an overdose.

I unclench my shoulders and roll my head back and forth across the pillow to get the knots out of my neck. Tomorrow is his birthday. Birthdays are important. No matter how sick, or strung out, or broke, you have to remember a birthday. For my nineteenth, he got take-out Indian and gave me a TV, and even though we couldn't afford cable, it got decent reception, enough for my favorite shows.

He's a poet; he'll appreciate a birthday poem. I could write only a couple of silly lines. *Blow up balloons, it's Michael's day.*

Light the candles, time to play. Fine for a three year old, pitiful for a real poet. He deserves a real poem. There's probably one in his books I can copy. For his birthday dinner, some Southern cooking to remind him of home, like corn pudding, collards with bacon. I'll fry some chicken. Sweet potato pie—he loves that more than any kind of cake. What is the recipe . . . two potatoes, two eggs, a cup of sugar. Cinnamon, nutmeg . . .

I MUST HAVE slept because Patty's "Ma! Ma!" wakes me. When I open the door to her bedroom, she's bouncing from foot to foot, showing all six of her teeth, her hair a fuzzy halo. Patty's skin is warm, rosy. She reeks of pee. "Phew, you need a bath," I say.

"Not? Not?" Her word for milk. She pats my face. She has Michael's eyes, wide-set, dark blue. Clear, though, not hard stones like his.

I fix a bottle and take her to our bed where she sucks it down, kicking rhythmically against the mattress. She's been doing that since she was born, practically, slamming her legs to make her crib mobile shimmy and dance. I couldn't believe a little baby could be that smart. Now the kicking is a habit. Even one-year-olds can have a habit.

I boil water for her oatmeal and plop her into her high chair. She feeds herself, getting about half the oatmeal into her mouth and the rest on her hair, her red T-shirt. Then it's bath time in the kitchen sink. She splashes, smacking the water until I'm soaked and we're laughing. I love this time of day. Fooling around with a no-worries baby, I'm almost happy.

Patty is the only shiny new thing in our apartment. A sheet covers a used couch. Michael found our mattress at the Salvation Army, and I layered blankets over it because you never know who slept on it or what they did when they weren't sleeping. He has sold everything else, most of his books and the TV he gave me for my birthday. Didn't get good reception, he said.

I spread a sheet on the floor for Patty and her toys, and sit down to play with her. She loves to look at my photo album, a record of better days, back when I had hope and a camera. It opens to our wedding picture. I was pregnant, but didn't show, and pretty enough, with shining hair and a dimpled smile. But Michael, he was gorgeous, with broad shoulders and intense blue eyes that flashed with a wicked wit. The two of us were like a pair of cardinals, the female a mousy brown, invisible next to the male's gleaming scarlet and black trimmings. When we were together, no one looked at me, except to wonder how I caught him, how I held him.

I wondered the same, at first. He was an actor, a poet, a musician, far out of my league. I was working as a waitress at a pizzeria in Woburn when he came in for lunch. He carried a book by Seamus Heaney, District and Circle.

"A poet," I said. "I've heard of him." I slipped his pizza onto the table.

He looked surprised. "You've heard of Heaney?" He was cute but that look and that question were not compliments. I recognized belittlement. Fourteen years in foster care made sure of that. I slapped the check on the table. "Have a nice day." I turned away.

He waited outside for me and invited me to a play the next night that he was acting in. "As You Like It, have you seen it? I know you've heard of it, I won't make that mistake again." He was brilliant on stage, funny, with great timing and a presence like he'd been born there. He asked me to the after-show party and introduced me all around. It was a night I'll always remember, the energy of the people, the talk, Michael's lively heat.

I turn the album page to a picture of his band mates, taken about the time they started up, playing gigs for free. They weren't half bad, but not great, not exactly Guns 'N Roses, except in the drugs department, where they competed on a level with Adler and Slash. The band broke up after a year and I wasn't sorry—I was sick of them. Right before Patty was born, I fixed them all dinner, a dinner that ended with spaghetti everywhere as, one by one, they—including Michael—passed out and their plates slid to the floor. Then they took him off for a day to "practice," but it was three days before he came home strung out and only wanting to sleep. After that, I locked the door when any of that miserable lot showed up.

I shove the album under the sofa. I can't stand to remember my old self, aging out of foster care, shy and naive. I'd been eligible for college funds until I got pregnant. Knocked up at eighteen, sentenced to life.

If you deal with assholes, all you get is shit, Brandi would say. I close my eyes to hear the rough jokey voice of my only friend. *Get it together, girl. You can't polish a turd.* Was she calling Michael a turd? I smile. Get it together, starting with the crap on the floor and the table. I can't think straight in all this mess.

I sort our clothes into the laundry basket or the closet, then clear the dishes off the table and into a pan of soapy water. Pitch the empty beer bottles, cigarette butts, candy wrappers. I scoop up a stack of mail and sort through bills we can't pay, the rest junk, except for a letter to Michael from the hospital.

Welcome to. The details of your employment etc. Your benefits are. Sick days, vacation, life insurance, health, dental. Sincerely. I read the letter twice. His job is a lifeline off a tilting shipwreck onto solid ground. If only he can keep it. He has a good attitude and can bullshit with the best of them. Showing up on time, going the distance—that's his trouble.

A box beside our bed holds his books. He loves poetry, he reads it aloud to me, but still I'm surprised he hasn't sold the books yet. I open them one by one—Larkin, Yeats, Frost, Heaney—leafing through for a birthday poem. Finally, in a collection by Sylvia Plath, I discover "A Birthday Present." Perfect.

What is this, behind this veil, is it ugly, is it beautiful?
It is shimmering, has it breasts, has it edges?

The speaker, making pastry, wants something for her birthday. I read the poem three times and can't figure it out. Michael always says I am too literal. Does her cooking stand for the creation of the poem? I copy it onto blank paper. The ending is shivery:

There would be nobility then, there would be a birthday.
And the knife not carve, but enter
Pure and clean as the cry of a baby,
And the universe slide from my side.

Is that what she wants for her birthday, a knife?

AT NOON I carry Patty across the hall. The floor plan of Brandi's two bedroom is identical to mine, but otherwise it's a different world, with coffee-colored walls, chairs that match, and a cootie-free couch with a tapestry cover. Plants in the window and a lovely fresh smell. I sniff. "Mmm, what is it?"

"A cleaner I mixed up—vinegar, water, and lemon juice," Brandi says, her voice raspy and hoarse. It's the voice that's carried me through the past year, and it still works. Brandi has a book in front of her—she's taking courses at Bunker Hill. "Have a seat, girl. I need grown-up talk. Evan? Patty's here." Brandi is pregnant, about five months, and it suits her—she is plump and calm, her skin fine and glowing. Her hair is in rollers to straighten it.

Evan tears himself away from *Bob the Builder* on TV and flings himself at Patty. "Boo! Boo!" he says and she reaches out and grabs his hair. "Yow!" he screams, delighted, bumping her belly with his head.

"Can you do me a big favor and watch Patty tomorrow night?" I ask. "It's Michael's birthday and I'm getting tickets to see Vinnie Paz at the Paradise."

"Sure, no problem."

"I'll watch Evan Saturday morning for you. You can study. Going out?" I point to the rollers.

"Got a math test tonight. Wish me luck." She rolls her eyes but I know she'll ace it, she always does.

"I'd love to go back to school."

"Someday." Brandi squeezes my hand.

"Somewhere, rainbow, bluebirds." I suddenly feel like crying and stand up before it happens. "I gotta catch the bus. Thanks, hon." I drop two diapers on the table and kiss Patty, who ignores me, her crystal eyes glued to the screen, admitting all the mush, unfiltered. Spud is playing tricks on Scoop.

The bus is crowded and I stand the whole way, twenty minutes of jerky stop-and-go. My feet ache. My polyester uniform feels greasy, with a smoky smell that won't wash out.

Jerry's Barbeque has a limited menu—slaw, French fries, pie, and pulled pork—but plenty of people eat there, especially the ones who are allergic to anything green. I welcome the chat with regulars, refilling their coffee cups. After the dinner rush, I go into the storage room and start to count my tips. When Jerry comes in, I quickly shove the money into my apron pocket to free up my hands. He's a goddam pest, always groping the girls from behind, leaning into them. He scatters us like a cat in a flock of juncos, but this time I'm alone and cornered.

"Coral the adorable." He tilts into me. His hairy arms are strong, and he pins me against the wall, shoves himself between my thighs. I push him away, jam my knee up, hard. He gasps and backs off. I grab a knife off the counter and stab the air. "I'll cut it off, you jerk." He reaches for my hand, the one holding the knife, and as we struggle, I feel the knife slice my palm.

Sharp. A lot of blood. I howl and Jerry jumps back. Warm blood runs down my fingers, but I don't take my eyes off him. His smarmy expression is gone and his breath is noisy. "Hey," he says, "just kidding around. Guess I'll have to fire you now."

"Do it. Do us both a favor." My heart bounces in my chest. I want to slide the knife into him, right into his gut, rip him open like hari-kari. He reads my face and backs away, turns to go. I reach out and wipe my injured hand on him. He hurries out of the room with a bright red smear on the back of his shirt.

"*Fuck* you," I holler after him. I wrap a clean dish towel around my hand. I'm exhilarated and a little dizzy from pain and the power of the knife. I put it in my pocket, it's mine now, and useful, as Jerry seems to respect it. I close the door to the storage room and slide a carton of paper towels in front of the door. I'm trembling, not from fear but adrenaline, and I feel pretty good. Fuck him.

Sitting down on the box, I count my tips. Eighty-four dollars, excellent. Enough for Michael's birthday present and some left over for diapers.

On the way home, I stop at the Paradise and buy two tickets for the concert.

MICHAEL'S TRUCK IS gone and our apartment is dark. Shit. That means Brandi still has the baby. I tap on her door, gently so I don't wake anyone. Brandi lets me in. Patty is asleep on the couch.

"Sorry," I whisper. "Michael didn't pick her up?"

Brandi shakes her head. "I gotta talk to you. It's trouble time, girl. Let's go to your place."

I don't want to know about any trouble, I can't take any more. I'm so exhausted I could sink onto the floor and sleep for a week. I ease Patty into her crib, then collapse onto the sheet-covered couch. Didn't I clean up this morning? Dishes and toys litter the room. The trash bin has been tipped over, mess everywhere. "What happened?"

"Michael got Patty around three. About an hour later, I heard her in the hall, crying."

"In the hall?"

"I look out, and all hell's broken loose. Your door is open, and there's Knotty Knickers holding the baby. Michael's passed out on your sofa."

Dear Jesus, that's bad. Knotty Knickers is what we called Barbara Knicker, the social worker. DCF has been shadowing me ever since I aged out of foster care and got pregnant. Along with food stamps, I'm apparently entitled to my very own social worker.

"Knotty wanted to talk to you. Your door was wide open so she went in. Patty was into the garbage over there and Michael wouldn't wake up. I told her you'd be home any minute now, I'd take care of the baby until then."

DCF almost took my baby? I shudder, knowing what that meant. Once they take your child, it's hell getting her back. Hearings and interviews and urine tests. Judges and social workers. And Michael being what he is . . . "What did Knotty say? Is she coming back?"

"She'll be back Monday." Brandi places her cool hands on my cheeks and turns my face until our eyes lock. "You can't leave Patty with him. Ever."

I rub my forehead. I'm tired yet every nerve twangs. "I know, but what can I do?" I feel sweat break out all over, and stand to unzip my uniform. It has a side zipper, it's hard to take off. "Help me," I say, and Brandi tugs the uniform over my head.

"What's this?" She's found the knife.

I tell her the story, embellishing only a little. "I kneed him in the nuts! Told him I'd slice his pecker off!"

Brandi squeals and pumps her arm in a victory salute. "You go girl! You are gutsy!"

"It felt *so* good. He knew I'd do it too." I pull one of Michael's tee-shirts out of the laundry basket and put it on.

"Hey, maybe you can use it to cut the knots. Get it? Knotty? Knots?" Though Brandi smiles, her eyes are worried.

I SLEEP LIKE a dead person all night, and don't wake until the baby calls. I open my eyes—I'm alone in the bed. Michael is talking to her; he must have come in during the night. I stretch. It's lovely to lie in bed though my hand feels sore. A bit of blood has leaked through the bandage onto my nightgown.

"Not? Not?" I hear Patty ask, then Michael brings her into our bedroom with a bottle. He leans down and kisses my forehead. He's shaved and he smells like soap. He doesn't look sick, so he must have gotten money somewhere.

"Glad to see you, babe," I say. "Happy birthday." He smiles. Once upon a time, that little curl to his mouth made me melt, made me want to lick him all over. "Where were you last night?" Patty drinks her milk, her crystal blue eyes moving from me to him, kicking her legs up and slamming them down on the bed.

He winces. "You don't want to know. It was rough." He lies down to face us.

I squeeze his shoulder, run my hand down his arm. I love his body, like a sleek animal's. "Be home tonight? I have a birthday surprise for you."

"You're an angel." He kisses me again, this time on the mouth, a lingering kiss that sends a charge from head to toe. Something to be thankful for.

"Knickers came by yesterday," I say.

He looks blank. "When?"

"Before I got home. Michael, she almost took Patty!"

"Why?"

"You were out of it, according to Brandi. Asleep."

"Fuck, I'm sorry."

He has a kicked-puppy look. Are those tears in his glazed, dead eyes? I don't feel pity. When do I get to cry? "Go to work, okay?"

"Sure, no worries." He half-smiles, squeezes my feet.

It will be a good day—no bus, no Jerry, no greasy pork and fries. I re-bandage my hand—the wound looks clean. I make a cup of ginger tea, feed Patty oatmeal and cooked apple, and decide to think positive about Knickers. The rent is due today so I dig in my old parka at the back of our closet for the Band-Aid tin where I keep my tip money. Money for food, rent and laundry, never enough.

The tin is empty.

A wave of panic dizzies me and I close my eyes until the spinning stops. I turn the parka pocket inside out, feel around on the closet floor. Nine hundred and forty-eight dollars, three weeks of serving up greasy fries and burned pork and slabs of lemon meringue pie, smiling at the ten percent tips, dodging old coots who want a hug. All gone.

I pull myself onto the bed, feeling weirdly numb and disconnected. Is this the worst that could happen? No. The worst is ahead of me. I have fourteen dollars. Michael doesn't get paid for two more weeks. We'll have to live in his truck. Knickers will take the baby.

I check the Vinnie Paz tickets—non-returnable. Perhaps I can go to the Paradise, stand around in the parking lot, scalp them. Be calm, think. *Get it together, girl.*

WHEN PATTY GOES down for a nap, I take the chicken out of the fridge and carve it into pieces, using the utility knife I filched from the restaurant. The knife slices sweetly through the skin, the meat, the tendons, effortlessly. I dip each piece in egg, then flour, sprinkle the pieces with salt and pepper and slide them into sizzling fat. I rehearse what I might say to him. *Sugar. Got any ideas regarding the rent? What about your truck payment?* As I scrape the sweet potatoes, sending the peelings flying into the sink, I imagine his hurt puppy look, his silence.

I read the Sylvia Plath poem again, out loud this time, but softly, so I won't wake Patty. Some lines I read twice: *I would not mind if it were bones, or a pearl button.*

Bones, like a skeleton. *I think it wants me.* I like the sound of the words.

MICHAEL EXCLAIMS OVER the concert tickets, the meal, the poem. He reads it out loud and laughs. "This is perfect, baby. It means more than you know. Sylvia Plath on my birthday."

Feeling generous, I smile at him. I watch Michael eat. He's gentle and funny, yummy-looking, with his long legs and dark hair that flops in his eyes and makes me want to push it up over his forehead. I remember our early days when just scrambling eggs together, or walking in the woods, I'd lean against him and feel blissful and safe. How his hands trembled when he reached for me, the peppery taste of his skin.

But his looks are like varnish sprayed over termite-riddled wood, shine over rot. A ghost picking at a chicken thigh.

IT'S TIME TO leave for the concert. I borrow some of Michael's clothes—a long-sleeved tee-shirt, a flannel shirt, a camouflage jacket. I don't want to attract attention, where there will be five guys for every girl.

On the way Michael makes a stop at an apartment complex I don't recognize. He jogs into the building to buy drugs. When he comes back, I ask what he bought.

"Got me some E. Gotta have it for the mosh. You'll mosh with me, won't you? It'll be awesome." He loves the mosh pit, the pushing, head-banging, body-surfing. The uncontrolled violence where anything could happen.

At the arena, Michael shoves his way in, past tattooed skateboard kids, death-rockers, bikers, dazed surfer dudes. He drags me up to the front. A strong smell of weed makes me queasy. As the overhead lights dim, roving spotlights picks up the ripple of swaying bodies. When the band starts, the music is so amplified that my ribs vibrate, my head feels muffled in sound. An explosion booms from the stage, pocketed with bursts of white flame. At first we are on the edge of the mosh, then it engulfs us. Bodies bump me, their elbows prod.

I slip behind Michael and put my arms around his waist, tug on his arm until he leans down. "Happy birthday, baby," I say into his ear. He can't hear me, he is shouting, possessed by the crowd's energy and the drug and the noise. He's so thin I can count his ribs, feel his heart pulsing. All around us the crowd writhes and lurches. I slip my bandaged hand into my jacket pocket and feel the knife, wrapped in a small towel. Someone is being passed overhead, hand to hand, and he kicks Michael in the head. Michael staggers but the crowd holds him upright. I press myself to him and hold him tight, hold on to my sweet boy's life.

The Years of the Wicked

THIS WARD'S LIKE Death Row, all of us in line for the big compost pile. Can't stand the waiting. Or the noise. Beep, drip, whoosh. Who knew I'd end up hooked to machines? Sometimes it's hard to hear the TV. I like *48 Hours* and *Cops*. Bad boys, bad boys . . . Someday they'll make a movie about my last case but I'll never watch it. I'm sliding to eternity too fast. Damn. I'd like to see that movie, find out what I've forgotten.

One thing I've learned recently, talking helps me remember. See, even us old guys can learn, something Rhianna wouldn't believe. "You're a rigid thinker, John," she'd say. An ex-wife can get bitter and say unkind things. But I don't play that game. It could get back to our daughter that I'd said something mean about her mother, and I'm already on eggshells with that one. She just turned fifteen, kind of another rigid thinker.

The paint hasn't dried on my last case. It irks me that the headlines blazed "Serial Killer!" It terrified the citizens of our quiet town, a fine place to live if you've got nerves, like I do. In my twenty-nine years on the police force, we never had a single homicide until that one bloody week.

The first death looked like a mugging. Early Sunday morning, Sam Klinkevals—a lawyer known for sucking lifeblood out of the gullible—looked out the back window of his office and saw a body in the alley. Once Sam figured out there was no profit in it for him, he called the cops.

I don't work Sundays but I've always got the scanner on, another thing that drove Rhianna nuts, out of the house, and into the arms of that scrawny accountant. I'd just come back from visiting my Momma's grave when the static broke and Drum's shaky voice said, "10-54, possible dead body." I pulled on my uniform and drove to the crime scene.

The body—really dead, not just possible—was a sixtyish male, a little soft around the middle like most of us. He lay face up, staring at a row of garbage pails. His nose had been relocated and his face was bloody, so he didn't look like himself, but I knew him. I pulled up his jacket sleeve to show Drum a fading tattoo, a bulldog just like mine. Semper Fi, another Marine. I'd met him the night before. His name was Roman Falco.

I'd been chewing the fat with the bartender, a good buddy of mine, in Nam about the same time as me; he'd been a chopper pilot and I was infantry. That history marks you, gives you a bond. When Falco walked up, we saw the tattoo, and the three of us had a drink together, playing who-did-you-know and where-were-you-at. Hell, we even joked about post-traumatic stress and who had it worst. I won with my story about the time a helicopter flew overhead and set off a flashback, and I locked Rhianna in the bathroom for a day while I stood guard against the hordes of Cong yelling outside our front door. That was the first time Rhianna threatened to leave me, though I didn't brag about that.

Chief Jerry asked me to find out more about the dead guy. It wasn't hard. His car keys came from an agency at the airport; I advised them we'd have to impound the car and they wouldn't get it back for a while. Notebooks and binders in the car told me Falco was traveling through, selling aluminum windows. I found a key to the Town Motor Lodge and went over there to check out his room. Just clothes, a ditty bag, a Ludlum thriller—nothing to suggest a motive for a murder.

Falco's body went to the morgue. The medical examiner said he'd been killed when a single punch drove his facial bones into his brain. He'd been drunk, blood alcohol content of 0.13, which didn't help his reflexes.

Two days later we were still investigating the Falco murder when the leech lawyer Sam Klinkevals killed himself. At least that's what it looked like—he was in his car in his garage, car windows down, garage door shut, engine running until it quit when the car ran out of gas. Sam's wife found him around noon and called 911. I was on patrol and got there in minutes.

She'd pulled Sam onto the garage floor. He was already stiff, bright pink from the carbon monoxide. He was dressed in his usual black suit, white shirt, striped tie—undertaker clothes, suitable for someone always delivering bad news. He'd been Rhianna's divorce lawyer, a contributor to a very sorry chapter in my life. His wife went into the house to look for a suicide note but I waited with the body. I didn't mind. I saw plenty of bodies in Nam. I'm not superstitious about them, though I stood behind so his eyes weren't aiming at me.

The medical examiner pronounced carbon monoxide poisoning as the cause of death, wrote "suicide" on the death certificate, and that's where it rested, until the next day, when the mayor was stabbed to death in her garage.

The mayor's son called the police station in hysterics. I got him to stop snuffling long enough to tell me his mother had been hurt. I paged Chief Jerry, because I knew the mayor was her friend. She was getting her hair done and said she'd be there soon. Oh yeah, Chief Jerry's female. Built like a shoebox with a bit of a mustache, but still, a female. My buddies kidded me about being replaced by a woman, but I was glad to give it up. Any time a citizen didn't like my style, I'd hear about it from town hall. She's better than I was at the personal stuff. She knows the right words.

The mayor's house was in the historic district, in a colonial full of cats. Her son led me into the garage. He wasn't fond of me, remembering the times I'd driven him home against his will because I knew his mother didn't want him associating with riff-raff. Well, now he could associate with anyone he wanted to since his mother lay face down on the garage floor. I felt for a pulse in her neck, then lifted an eyelid to check her pupil.

"She's dead, isn't she?" the boy said. His face crumpled and tears spilled out of his eyes. I told him I understood, that my mom had died recently so I knew how hard it was. Momma was eighty-four years old, living on her own, gardening and playing cards right up until she went into the hospital. Maybe she didn't feel so great, since she was nearly dead by the time the doctors finally figured out what was wrong. That's water under the bridge, though I wished the boy wasn't the one to find his mother's body.

By the time Chief Jerry arrived, I had taped off the garage and started dusting for fingerprints. She looked prettier with her hair streaked blonde, but the moment wasn't right to mention it. I *can* be sensitive, contrary to public opinion.

She knelt by the body and touched the mayor's hand. "She was a good person. Makes you believe in evil."

I shivered. Momma would have said someone was walking over my grave. "It's the second homicide this week," I said.

"I'm going to ask the State Bureau of Investigation for help. We need someone to direct the lab work and talk to the medical examiner. When's the last time you read an autopsy report, John?"

"Umm, never?" I was trying to decide which of about a thousand greasy fingerprints to lift from the door.

"The SBI can get bank and cell phone records. Background checks. Credit card transactions. We don't have those resources." Her voice trembled, and for a second I thought she might cry. She took a few deep breaths and made the call to Raleigh. Females, they're tough as Marines sometimes.

THAT AFTERNOON, DRUM and I were at our desks when we heard a car pull up. We looked out the plate glass window, like we always did, to see who it was. A dark-haired woman not much older than my daughter got out of a Dodge Intrepid. She opened the car's back door and took out a briefcase and a red jacket.

Drum whistled. "Well, lookee that."

"Don't whistle. Makes us look like pea brains."

"Nice skirt," he said. It was leather and showed lots of leg. We watched her slide on the red jacket. A weapon glinted in her shoulder holster.

"She's armed," I said. "Bet she's with the SBI."

She was. She handed out her card. *Stella Lavender, Special Agent, Field Operations Division, North Carolina State Bureau of Investigation.* At first I thought—here's a dollar, go buy the rest of your skirt. The thought lasted two seconds. She shook everyone's hand and asked to see our reports, to take with her to the hospital where she was going to talk to the medical examiner.

And while she was gone, would we interview everyone who knew the mayor? In other words, get up off our duffs. Furthermore, she was extending the investigation to include the deaths of Sam Klinkevals and Roman Falco. Chief Jerry and I exchanged looks—what had we missed? I shrugged and hit the streets.

Around noon, I stopped in the barbershop for a trim. Not much grows up there, but I like it tidy. Besides cutting hair, the barber also dabbled in housing development, and I knew he'd fought with the mayor on zoning and watershed protection— two issues that came up with each new development in Simms Fork. When he finished snipping, I asked him if he planned to attend the mayor's funeral.

"Oh yeah. I'll miss her, even though she was a pain in the ass. If she'd had her way, there'd be not a single new house built, ever." The barber was red-faced from resentful thinking. "But I sure am sorry to hear she's dead." He didn't sound very sincere. He had an airtight alibi; he'd been at the hospital for a colonoscopy. "Clean as a whistle," he said.

I congratulated him on his shiny colon and was nearly out the door when my cell phone rang. I listened for a minute. "How do you know this? Who are you?" I asked, but heard only a dial tone.

I called Chief Jerry. "Some news. I just got an anonymous call from a female informant. She said Turk Holmes mugged Falco and there's evidence at his house." I headed to Turk's place on Elm Street.

Turk spent his days drinking Old Crow bourbon diluted with Dr. Pepper, what they call bug juice. He liked to wander though I always tried to keep him out of the better neighborhoods. He'd get mellow, fall asleep somewhere, no harm done. He lived with his mother. Mrs. Holmes' yard was respectable, neatly planted with little pink flowers, and the statuary included several plaster angels. No doubt Mrs. Holmes needed considerable angelic assistance where Turk was concerned.

Turk was alone with a thirty-six-inch TV blaring ESPN. Ten years ago, he'd lettered in football, basketball, and track, but his senior year he dropped out of school, working a day here and there to earn money for his bug juice. He still had an athletic build, but I could smell the alcohol on him, and he looked puffy, with bloodshot eyes. I told him to sit on the couch and stay there. I wasn't too worried about Turk. He usually did what he was told.

I looked around the small house—four rooms on one floor—and started to rummage in Turk's bedroom, still papered with football posters and a framed autographed picture of Michael Jordan. Within a minute I found a black leather wallet, stuffed under the mattress. It still held Falco's license and credit cards. The missing car keys turned up in a dresser drawer, under a pile of T-shirts.

I went back into the living room. "Were you planning to use these credit cards? Assume his identity? You don't look much like him."

He slid his jumpy eyes from the TV and tried to focus on the evidence bags. "What you talking about? I never seen that shit before."

I read him his Miranda rights, and he responded yeah yeah. As liquored up as he was, it was unlikely he understood, so I decided to wait and question him after he'd dried out some. I arrested him for possession of stolen goods. A few months in jail might do him some good. He'd dry out, maybe get religion, think about where he was going.

After I brought Turk to the police station, Chief Jerry asked me to find Ben Lacker and talk to him. A certified loony, Ben marched the streets ten hours a day clutching a beat-up canvas suitcase and reciting Scripture. Though Ben scared the bejesus out of most of the citizens, it escaped me how he could be a suspect. He was harmless as a fruit fly.

Ben was home, eating a nice dinner, fried chicken with mashed potatoes and black-eyed peas. His suitcase stood between his feet, under the table.

"It's his birthday today, the big four-oh," his sister said. Edie was a nurse, a freckly redhead in her mid-forties.

"Happy birthday, Ben." I leaned down to catch his gaze and he glared back at me, grease from the chicken coating his chin.

"Whoso diggeth a pit shall fall therein, and he that rollest a stone, it will return upon him." He spoke in round gloomy tones, not easy when your mouth is full of fried chicken.

"Hey, just being friendly." I turned to Edie. "Sounds like a retribution theme?"

"Could be. That and salvation are his favorites."

"Has he been good about his medication lately?"

"Why? Someone complain?"

I noticed the tiny wrinkles etched into her forehead and around her eyes, the skin drooping around her mouth. I didn't know how she kept doing it, looking out for Ben, checking him into the hospital when his rambling turned delirious, nagging him to take his meds. "No, Edie. Can you just answer the question?"

"He's been good as gold." She stood up. "Listen, I'm going to change out of this uniform. Keep him company?"

"Sure," I said. I wondered if Ben would share his chicken. It smelled good. But I didn't want to rile him up by asking. I looked around at the combination living-dining room, furnished with two worn recliners, a TV, and a bookcase containing Edie's nursing books and several hundred romance novels with lurid flowery covers. Rhianna hated romance novels. She once found one in our daughter's room. I said if that's the worst you find, you're lucky, but she called it propaganda for the witless, and threw it into the trash can.

"Ben, did you know the mayor?" I asked. I felt a bit guilty asking him about the murder—he couldn't know the risk of telling me anything—but I'd never really talked with him and wasn't sure how much he understood.

"The years of the wicked shall be shortened," Ben declared. He put down his fork and wiped his hands on a napkin. "All go unto one place; all are of the dust, and all turn to dust again."

Now, that answer almost fit. "You know, I wonder what's in that suitcase?" I asked. He always clutched it tightly, as if the contents were precious.

"Evil pursueth sinners, but to the righteous good shall be repaid." He hoisted it onto his lap and unfastened the buckles. It was full of paper, like magazine pages, all folded neatly into little square wads.

"Aha. Paper weighs a lot—is it heavy?"

Ben lifted it high to show me how light it was, then put it back under the table and returned to his dinner.

"Light as a feather. Are they pictures, or special articles you cut out?" I asked.

"Whoso causeth the righteous to go astray in an evil way, he shall fall himself into his own pit; but the upright shall have good things in possession."

"Good things. Okay. Speaking of good, that chicken looks real good."

Ben pushed the plate over to me, and I picked out a drumstick. "I don't get much home cooking any more. This is great," I said. We crunched companionably until Edie returned. I asked her when Ben usually started walking each day. She wasn't sure since she left for work at six thirty. I thought about Ben's speechifying and wondered what had triggered the vengeance theme.

She took Ben into another room to give him a shot. While they were gone, I pulled a few of the paper wads out of the suitcase and unfolded them. They were pictures of things Ben would never have—expensive cars and pretty girls. Pretty girls *in* expensive cars. Maybe he wasn't as devout as he seemed.

THAT EVENING WE met with the SBI Agent, Stella Lavender. Chief Jerry had ordered out for pizza and sodas, but Stella said she'd already eaten and would just drink her water. She wore a black suit with another short skirt. She sat on the table and crossed her legs, and her skirt slid a few inches higher. I think Drum stopped breathing for a while there.

"You all knew the mayor. Tell me what she was like," Stella said.

We looked at each other to see who would go first. Chief Jerry spoke up. "She was hardworking. She volunteered for everything—the women's center, the nursing home, church bake sale."

"A good community citizen," I said. "On the other hand . . ." I took a bite of pizza so my mouth would be full and looked at Drum, hoping he'd finish my sentence.

"She could be a bitch," he said. "Sticking her nose in. Her way or the highway. At least that's what we saw in the department."

"She wanted changes?" Stella took a swig from her water bottle.

"She wanted a lower-profile department," I said. I didn't mention the time the mayor called me a fascist. It had been a heated moment, not reflecting the best in either of us.

"Meaning . . ." Stella said.

"Kinder, gentler cops," I said.

Stella studied me. Her eyes were the green of shallow seas. "I understand there was an arrest today in the Falco killing?"

"Turk Holmes. He had Falco's wallet and keys hidden at his house," I said.

"Do you think he killed Falco?"

I was beginning to realize how easy it was to underestimate this young woman. You couldn't tell what she was thinking, for one thing. She had the same calm, serious expression whether she was sipping water or asking a question you couldn't answer.

"I don't know. He could have picked those items up from someone else. I have to wait until he sobers up to interview him," I said.

Stella tapped her pencil on the table. "Our killer likes garages. Two murders in a garage."

"Two?" I asked.

"Sam Klinkevals was murdered. Tied up and gassed in the trunk of his car. This morning I took a closer look at the body, and found duct tape residue on his wrists."

"Don't know how I missed that," I said.

"We see the evidence that supports our assumptions," said Stella.

"No motive, no suspects," said Drum. "Doesn't look very promising."

Stella shook her head. "That's pessimistic. Let's put it this way—there's no obvious suspect, yet. If we do our jobs right, though, we'll nail him. I have no doubt at all about that." She finished her water and slid off the table. The meeting was over.

I followed Chief Jerry into her office. "What do you think?" I asked.

"About the murders?"

"Yeah."

"I think she'll solve them. I pray she will. No one around here is sleeping very well."

"She married?"

Chief Jerry frowned. "She's too young for you, John."

"Give me a break. I think Drum likes her."

"Well, I don't know if she's married. And her personal life doesn't have anything to do with the job."

"Sure, no need to be testy."

"Sorry," she said, smiling. She should smile more often—it gives her dimples.

ALL WEEKEND, DRUM and I interviewed a good slice of the townsfolk. We heard gossip, accusations, suspicions. We took notes, compared theories, and reported back to Chief Jerry. She and Stella were working on leads the SBI had uncovered.

On Sunday night, Edie Lacker walked into the police station and heaved Ben's worn suitcase onto the counter. When Chief Jerry opened the suitcase and saw what was underneath the hundreds of folded-up squares, she had Ben arrested and put into a cell.

The next afternoon, I found Edie going into the jail to visit Ben. She looked pale, more tired than usual, with her hair pulled back by a leopard-print headband. She told me what happened. "Ben was sorting through his pictures, like he does sometimes. I was washing dishes and he came into the kitchen. He was holding this bloody knife and saying something like 'the wicked shall fall by his own wickedness,' the kind of stuff I usually ignore, but when it's your crazy brother with a bloody knife in his hand it takes on a different meaning."

"How's he doing?" I asked.

"He doesn't mind being here right now," Edie said, "though he's going to be frustrated tomorrow when he can't walk around town. The blood on the knife is the mayor's, you see. Ben stabbed her. I can't believe it!" She began to cry.

I found her a tissue. "He's innocent, even if he did it. He doesn't know what he did."

She groped through her bag and took out a pill bottle. "He's never harmed a soul. All these years, no matter how sick he got."

I stayed with her while she gave Ben his medicine. It was the least I could do, poor kid. He seemed calm enough, though he kept asking for his suitcase.

STELLA LAVENDER SPENT Tuesday morning holed up with Chief Jerry. It had been nine days since Falco's killing. Ben had been moved to the hospital psych ward. We'd interviewed Turk Holmes, but he swore he knew nothing about Falco's murder. Since we didn't have evidence or a witness to prove otherwise, the judge let his mother bail him out. Drum and I had written up dozens of interviews, none of them containing a crumb of useful information.

Around four o'clock, Stella came out of Chief Jerry's office, looking wiped out, with dark circles around her eyes. On an impulse, I asked her if she wanted to have a beer with me. Maybe she could relax and update me on the reports from the SBI.

She said that was a good idea, she'd meet me in an hour.

I went home and washed up, changed into one of my sports shirts and some khaki pants. Shaved and brushed my teeth, even. Rhianna would say I was really trying to make an impression. It's true, I was hoping for a good opinion. Stella made me nervous. She was smart, and smart women tend to see right through my bullshit to whatever's underneath. I didn't want pity, not from her.

We each ordered a light draft beer, and sat down in a booth. Stella had on a white jacket with the top two buttons undone. It felt good to be with a woman, even if she did make me nervous. She sat across from me, and I had those sea-green eyes all to myself.

"Any new developments?" I asked.

"We found a partial shoe print on Falco's jacket, on the back. Like he was kicked. Same shoe print that we found on the mayor's skirt and in Klinkevals's garage. Size ten Nikes." Her voice took on a sharpness I hadn't heard before.

"But Turk Holmes had Falco's wallet. Did he kick Falco?"

"Turk wears size thirteen. It wasn't his shoe print."

"I'm sure you checked Ben's shoes," I said.

"Ben Lacker didn't kill the mayor. Ben's prints were on the knife, but not bloody, not positioned the way they'd be if he'd held it to stab her."

"Where did he get the knife, then?"

"He doesn't remember or doesn't know."

I sipped my beer. "Looks like we're back to square one."

"No. I have a suspect. I'm just waiting for a fax that might give me the final piece of the puzzle."

I nearly choked. "You know?" I couldn't believe it, that she had solved all three killings. "Who is it?"

"I'll tell you when I get the fax," she said. I couldn't read her expression.

"How did you find out? Mind telling me, so I learn something here?"

"The killings didn't fit the pattern of a ritualized or sadistic serial killing. These three people were killed for a reason, by someone who knew them. So I looked into their dealings, their problems, their lives, to find someone who might have a grudge. Someone they cheated or misused, maybe long ago."

"Makes sense to me." My heart raced. Who was the suspect?

Chief Jerry came in, carrying a manila envelope. She hesitated when she saw me with Stella, but when I waved at her to join us, she slid into the booth next to me and handed Stella the envelope.

"It's the fax," Stella said. She pulled out a sheet of paper and studied it intently. She exchanged a nod with Chief Jerry, then drew her Sig and aimed it at my forehead. When she said, "John Norman, you're under arrest for first-degree murder," my life began to evaporate like the bubbles in my beer.

She continued with Miranda rights. I didn't resist—I fully believed Miss Ice-In-Her-Veins would have shot me right between the eyes. What's more, I didn't get what she was talking about. I just didn't know, because my memory has holes like one of Momma's crocheted snowflakes. Stella seemed to believe her accusations. I didn't, couldn't, though a nasty cold whisper was reminding me that I didn't remember most of Nam either. I had a pain in my chest and tasted metal, like I'd swallowed a lead pipe.

"Drum's in your apartment right now with a search warrant, picking up your size ten Nikes," said Chief Jerry.

I stood up but got dizzy so I sat down again. "I didn't do it." I took deep breaths to calm myself. The pain in my chest was getting worse, spreading down my arms.

Stella pushed her beer aside. "I think I know the story, John. You're a proud man, but that pride was eroded by a series of humiliations. It started when the mayor replaced you as Chief, after you harassed her son."

"That's bull," I said. "I treated him the same as any other punk."

"The mayor demoted you to patrolman. You drank more than ever, until Rhianna kicked you out and filed for divorce. Her lawyer, Sam Klinkevals, convinced the court to issue you a restraining order."

"Now he was an evil man." I remembered his lies, how the court wouldn't let me see my family.

"So now you've lost your status, your wife, your home. You blamed the mayor and Sam Klinkevals."

"Blaming isn't murder." I couldn't catch my breath. I must have looked bad because Chief Jerry asked me if I was okay. "My chest hurts like a son-of-a-bitch," I said. She pulled out her cell and called for an ambulance.

"Your mother passed away, and you're grieving. About all you have left," Stella went on—not that I could stop her, "is the friendship of a few guys like the bartender over there, other veterans, men who fought for our country and respect each other for it. Then Roman Falco walks into the bar. He was in your Marine platoon in Vietnam." She tapped the manila envelope. "This fax from Washington contains the details of your general discharge in 1973. You deserted during your tour, and hid out. The only reason you weren't court-martialed was that there was no point in making an example of you anymore, the war was over. You recognized Falco right away?"

I tasted that sourness that goes with about-to-vomit. "He had this tattoo, a Marine bulldog. He hadn't changed much. He recognized me. The bartender started blabbing bullshit about my two tours and a Purple Heart for being shot in the back, point man in a recon platoon. Falco just kept swallowing those tequila shots."

"Yes, and he'd tell someone," Stella said. "Falco could destroy the only shred of yourself worth respecting. So you stopped him, or punished him."

"It wasn't me," I managed to croak. "You're wrong."

"No, it all fits. I wondered when you botched the evidence collection in Sam Klinkevals's garage. Then, too conveniently, Falco's wallet turned up the first place you looked. By the way, you didn't get any anonymous informant call that noon in the barbershop. We checked your cell phone records. You must have set the alarm to go off so you could fake a call."

She didn't miss a *damn* thing. The day after Falco's death, I'd found his wallet and car keys in my jacket pocket. I didn't have a fucking clue how they got there. Had I picked them up in the bar? Chief Jerry didn't need to know I had the wallet and keys, it would only confuse things. "Finding" them in Turk's house made sense to me.

Adding her two cents, Chief Jerry said, "Edie Lacker says you visited her and Ben, and you were alone with Ben's suitcase. You planted the knife, right?"

I shook my head, no, but she was right—I'd found the bloody knife in my car after the mayor's murder. I thought someone was planting evidence on *me*. I needed to get rid of the knife, and I knew Ben wouldn't be convicted.

The EMTs arrived and loaded me onto a stretcher. "Good work," Chief Jerry said to Stella, and gave her a hug. It almost made me throw up, the sight of those two heads pressed together, a dark shiny braid and a bleached blonde helmet. A couple of know-it-all broads hugging over my almost-corpse.

THE SHRINK'S GOT a chin patch, like a tarantula. It really gets on my nerves. He makes me talk until I remember. Heart-pounding, sweat-dripping flashbacks. Klinkevals's beady eyes, his cheeks flattened by duct tape, as he writhed in the trunk of his car. The glistening pool of blood under the mayor's body. Falco's drunken smirk just before I knocked his lights out. It's horrible when these memories appear.

What calms me is thinking about Momma. I recall the day she died, right before Falco came to town. She was nothing but skin hanging on bones, and she couldn't talk. Still, it was like her to keep busy, and she was crocheting a snowflake for the Christmas craft sale at the church. I was reading the newspaper to her, about the weddings and babies, when she put down the hook and thread, rested her knobby hands in her lap, closed her eyes, and passed away.

I held together until the funeral. They say I recited Psalm 34 over Momma's coffin. *That* day I'd like to remember but the shrink isn't interested in respect for the dead. He wants me to open the coffin and hop right in with garages and knives and duct tape. I can't hold him down and rip off his chin patch like I want to, so I rattle my cuffs.

It makes him jump.

Gone Gone Gone

CELINE IS OUT grocery shopping, leaving me alone with her faithless lover. Brian squats on the fire escape as he talks to his latest girlfriend. He's surrounded by his swirly yellow aura, the color of self-regard. I crouch in the doorway, enjoying the evening breeze, the smells of the city. I'm thinking about Mom until I realize he is talking about me.

"Damn thing makes me sneeze. Cat hair everywhere. Tomorrow he's going for a ride. . . Yup, the Pound . . . Never did like cats, they belong in barns, not my bedroom . . . She'll get over it." He shoves me into the apartment with his foot.

I jump onto the top of the refrigerator to gather my thoughts. The Pound? The POUND? I can hear Mom's breathy hiss. *Where murder of our species is sanctioned.* Her aura had glowed red as fresh blood: the color of fear.

After I was born, Mom washed me clean and fed me from her teats. She carried me to a place of safety, a corner near a warm-air grate in an apartment building courtyard. There, knowing that my siblings and I would be adopted by the residents, she taught us basic survival strategies and the management of humans. She explained that most difficulties—an empty food dish, long-overdue cuddling, and distasteful litter box—could be resolved by a patient gaze, a judicious paw pat, or a quiet mew. And, of course, even the most oblivious human responds to an enthusiastic purr. But none of these lessons prepared me for Brian and his talk of the Pound.

Once, Celine and I lived together in utter contentment. I love Celine. She is kind, and her lap is warm. She buys the type of canned food I like, shreds. (The bits are too chewy and the pâté too, well, pasty.) Then Brian moved in. Right away I noticed his aura's sickly green fringe, the rude tone of his loud voice, his joking threats to turn me into a pair of slippers. His first night here, as I lay curled behind Celine's knees, Brian literally booted me out of the bedroom, an act of unnecessary violence that would have humiliated a less self-assured cat. I stifled a howl and found an alternative location, the top of the refrigerator. Which is where I am now, washing my soft fur. I am very clean. As I wash, I plot.

I am no victim. Mom instilled in me a sturdy feeling of self-esteem. Even though I am ordinary in my coloring—solid black except for a white heart-shaped patch on my chest—I am lifted above the common feline by the soft texture of my fur, my pale green eyes, and my imperturbable manner. Furthermore, I am blessed with unusual precognitive abilities, though should I be caught exercising them . . . well, one need only refer to the terrible history of atrocities visited on the cat, the result of ignorant superstition and myths. Centuries of persecution drove our species to disguise our powers, to express them with subtlety.

They think we are lower beings, Mom warned, *inadequate and limited. Let them believe that. No displays of cunning, ever.*

Mom would be proud. I have never allowed Celine to realize my gifts. She makes a fuss of my minor tricks—when I bring her one of Brian's balled-up cigarette packs for a game of fetch, or pull down on the handle to open the bathroom door. But does she notice that I distract her with playful jumps when Brian's on the fire escape phoning other women? My rumbly purr celebrating his absences? My leap onto the refrigerator one minute before he walks through the door? She does not, at least consciously.

Celine has returned from grocery shopping. Her aura is pale blue, reflecting a calm state of mind. Not for long, I fear. She changes into faded draw-string pants and a sweatshirt. She used to have more self-respect. I miss seeing her dance, fluidly gliding and twisting to the drums, the sweet thready flute. The one time she danced for Brian, he laughed unpleasantly, and she hasn't picked up her finger cymbals since.

The apartment is so tiny I can watch both of them from my perch. Admiring himself in the bathroom mirror, Brian sings along with the radio tuned to his favorite oldies station. "You're just too good to be true," he croons. He smiles at his mouthful of pure white teeth. He tilts his head this way and that, touches his slightly spiky gelled hair. "Can't take my eyes off of you." His singing makes my head hurt.

Celine sits on the couch and flips through the mail. She opens a credit card bill. "I thought we were going to try to save," she says without energy. "What's this four hundred dollars at Barney's? And the two-fifty?" Her aura is gray with streaks of green: sad with flashes of frustration.

He leans through the bathroom doorway. "Babe, Celine, the wing-tips, remember? And those Etro shirts you liked?"

"But we agreed. No needless spending. Especially on clothes. I'm not working double shifts to pay for shirts."

"Gotta look good in sales, Celine. You know that." Brian lies down on the bed as a ballad about fading love comes on the radio, inspiring him to sing along, " . . . cause it's gone, gone, gone." He punches the pillow with each "gone" and his aura momentarily pulses brown, then back to yellow. I slip into the bedroom and take one of my favorite spots on a pile of dirty clothes in the corner.

On the radio, an announcer says, "Stay tuned. Jackpot drawing coming up. Twelve million dollars, folks, and someone's gonna win, I have that feeling."

I'm feeling drowsy but a little tense. Something's going to happen. The air is charged.

Celine comes into the bedroom. "I need these clothes, mister." I submit limply to her kiss as her aura glows pinkly with affection. When she puts me down, I arch my back until every inch of my spine gets a good crack. She heaps the dirty clothes into a basket and I wander behind her to the closet where the washer and dryer are located. She sorts the clothes into two piles, lights and darks.

Feeling an impulse to stretch, I sprawl across the pile of lights—sheets, Brian's boxers and tee-shirts, dish towels. The pile makes a nice background for the striking blackness of my fur. Celine laughs and loads the machine with the other pile, emptying pockets of tissues, coins, and receipts.

I swipe at the trash basket until it tips over and spills its contents onto the floor. My attention has been caught by a bit of paper that must not be discarded. I bat it underneath the throw rug for safekeeping, then jump onto the dryer and wait.

The radio announcer sounds excited. "Now here's what you've been waiting for. Meet Sarah, the newest member of the Draw team. The jackpot tonight is twelve million greenbacks, folks. Someone's gonna win, I have that feeling. Here's Sarah . . ."

Brian listens intently as the balls fall and Sarah from the Draw Team recites each number. His aura has mutated from yellow to teal, the color of curiosity, and for an instant I feel a pang of loss. Teal was Mom's aura, except for the rare occasion when I was immature and she would flash purple with annoyance. It was a beautiful color combination.

"Thirty," Sarah begins.

"Good start," he mutters.

"Twenty-five."

He nods. "Cool."

"Sixteen."

He coughs and leaves his hand over his mouth.

"Thirteen."

"Oh. My. God."

"Fifty-four."

He pounds on the bed. "I don't believe it! A quarter million dollars!"

The announcer comes on. "One more ball, the Mega Ball. Tonight's Mega Millions—twelve million dollars. What's the number, Sarah?"

The sound of the rolling ball, then Sarah chirps, "Eleven."

"Hallelujah!" Brian whispers. "I'm rich! I'm rich forever! Woo hoo!" He stands and fist-pumps the air. His aura pulsates orange. It reminds me of the time Mom clawed the nose of a Rottweiler and sent him flying down the street yipping with fear. The aura of power and conquest. Brian opens the bedroom door and heads toward the fire escape.

Celine's lying on the sofa with a book and a glass of wine. I curl onto her warm lap. "Brian," she says, stroking my soft thick fur, "I need my credit card back. You'll have to get your own."

"Huh?" He looks at her distractedly then pulls out his wallet and hands her a card. "Yeah, sure. Listen, work's killing me. They want me on the West Coast. I'll be there a couple weeks. Where the hell are my new jeans?"

"I did wash. Maybe they're in the machine."

He stands still and stares at her for a beat. Then he turns and digs around in the washing machine until he finds a pair of soggy, twisted jeans. He holds them to his forehead as if saying a brief silent prayer, slips his fingers into a back pocket, and pulls out a small square of damp paper. It dissolves into fragments as he tries to unfold it. The ink is gone, it's unreadable. He searches in all the other pockets but comes up with nothing. He looks around, taking in the piles of clothing, the litter box, Celine in her wrinkled sweatshirt with me sprawled across her lap. "Friggin' unbelievable, a slob like you doing the laundry," he says. "Man, I'm outa here."

"To LA?" Celine asks.

"For good, baby. It's not working out for me."

Celine frowns and sits up, dislodging me from her lap. As her soggy gray aura pulsates, a line of silver—for hope—appears around its edges. I'm worried she'll beg him to stay. I remember his harsh words, kicks, threats to turn me into a pair of slippers. *The Pound.*

When Brian steps onto the fire escape and takes out his phone, I follow, winding around his legs, right there with him, affectionate-like, until he shoves me aside. I crouch next to a pot of dead marigolds. He closes the door and punches his phone. His aura is a cloudy black, streaked with gray. Odious.

Mom's martial instructions ring clearly in my head. *The eyes are defenseless. Go for the orbital sockets.*

I bound onto the railing then leap at his face, hooking a claw into each eyeball before he can react. My back claws dig into his neck, my teeth sink into his scalp. The furies of centuries possess me. Brian chokes out a shriek but quickly I tear into his throat to stifle it. When he knocks me away from his face I jump onto his leg, holding on with all twenty needle-sharp claws. He staggers, kicking, and I ride his foot as he lurches away, stumbling against the railing, then blindly down the wobbly metal stairs, losing his balance, somersaulting over the railing as I leap gracefully away to let him fall, down, down, down. Twelve stories. He lands on the sidewalk, inches from a sleeping drunken man. The two of them lie head to bloody head.

I take a deep breath and howl triumphantly, only once because Celine has opened the door. "Brian picks this time of night to leave?" she asks, frowning. "Oh well, good riddance. At least I got my Visa back." She picks me up and takes me inside.

My fur is awry. I hope up next to the sink and begin to wash my face, a displacement activity that calms my emotions. After a moment I am myself again. Celine has poured herself another glass of wine. Her aura is muddy brown swirled with a livid chartreuse, the colors of pessimistic befuddlement. She's thinking, "what's next?" and not seeing anything good. Time to fix that.

I retrieve the bit of paper that I'd hidden under the bathroom rug, and drop it at Celine's feet. She always exclaims how cute I look playing fetch, but this time, in her funk, she ignores me. I jump into the couch and drop it on her lap. She studies the paper, frowns, then her aura brightens. Glowing soft gold, she looks at me in wonder, a moment I'll remember for the rest of my life.

Kissing the slip of paper, Celine places it on the desk. She lights a candle, stands, and strips off her uniform to reveal a black bra and panties. She puts on a long red skirt embroidered with black flowers, slides a CD into the player and takes a pair of finger cymbals from her desk drawer. I hear the tickety-tock of drums, the sigh of a flute, and relax onto the floor to watch. Her aura is a brilliant aqua, the color of happiness, and I send a pulse of gratitude to Mom. Wherever she might be, she's proud of me tonight.

Lady Tremaine's Rebuttal

Castle-on-Wycks, Cardigan

MY LIFE IS bittersweet these days. Now that Ella, Anastasia, and Drizella are married and living in their own castles, it's quieter, even a bit lonely at times, though I've learned to cherish my solitude and enjoy special moments to myself like Sunday afternoons in my chamber, stretching out on the couch with the *London Times*. The dogs snore on the hearth, their feet twitching as they dream of chasing rats. Lord Tremaine's in his turret and won't descend until suppertime. The peacocks have wandered down to the pond, far enough away so their screams are muted. It's a lovely time for me, sipping my tea, nibbling a scone, alone with an excellent newspaper.

But today, when I pick up the Literary Supplement (leaving it for last, like dessert) I see, to my disgust, that the front page is devoted to my stepdaughter Ella's memoir, *Out of the Cinders*. Bile rises in my throat, burning and sour. Yes, the story's a classic: an inscrutable beauty, distant father, abusive stepmother, two ugly sisters. Rescue by a Prince, happily ever after, blah blah blah.

I am appalled that the *Times* has given credence to her pack of lies.

I wanted to love her. She was cute as a button, and motherless. She needed someone to pick the lice out of her hair and feed her something other than roast pigeon and watered-down mead. Her father is a dear man but the silent type, not one she could talk to. He spent most of his days in the southwest turret trying to prove Fermat's Last Theorem. If she'd given me half a chance we could've been friends.

It wasn't easy being Lady of the Manor. The castle was a crumbling wreck: tottery staircases, broken windows, a rat infestation that even our swarm of flea-ridden Jack Russells couldn't control. It was cold, and leaked in the rainy months. Blue fuzzy mildew grew on the tapestries. Drizella coughed all winter, and Anastasia had migraines. The servants weren't being paid and most of them had left, except the gamekeeper, a one-armed good old boy who made a tidy living selling the salmon out of our stream. The Lord and he nattered on for hours about nothing. It drove me crazy. To say I was disillusioned with my situation is an understatement. But as a wife and mother—my role, my lot, my choice—I did my best to make everyone comfortable and happy. I didn't complain, I tried to be fair.

The whole cinders thing is a complete fabrication. Ella had her own room, with a fireplace. On windy days a gust would come down the chimney and blow the cinders around. So she woke up with a dusting of ash now and then. We all did, but only Ella had the imagination to turn it into a pitiable moment.

She whines about her clothes. Well, there was too much to do, and no money. The girls had to pitch in, and that's where Ella and I clashed. She wouldn't do her chores. She slept late and mooned into mirrors and wept under the trees. So she didn't get her allowance. And, honey: no allowance, no dress! I couldn't afford a new ball gown every week! And the girl was mad for shoes. She wouldn't patronize the shoemaker—no, they had to be gold and copper and glass. I told her, you want shoes, you work for them. She screamed at me, called me a four-letter word. It wasn't l-a-d-y.

The incident of the Prince's ball is a perfect example of what I'm talking about. I spent the day helping all three girls with their hair, easing their jitters, reminding them about knees together. At suppertime Ella pitched a hypoglycemic fit, accusing me of poisoning her with the mushrooms in the stew. As her shrieks bounced from the rafters, Anastasia turned greenish like she does before a migraine. When I told Ella *indoor voice*, she dumped her stew on the floor. *No ball for you*, I said, *go to your room*. Don't you know she hitched a ride with a neighbor and went anyway? Mice, pumpkins, and fairy godmother—what an imagination! Guess it sells books.

She pranced into the ballroom and, not wasting a second on mere counts or earls, latched onto the Prince like a tick on a hound. Tugged her neckline a little too low, fluttered her lashes, and whispered something (dirty, no doubt) in his ear. When they disappeared to walk along the moat, the Queen was furious. She's still not speaking to me, though by now she's well aware of the futility of anyone's trying to manage that girl. In *Out of the Cinders* Ella writes that she left the ball at midnight, leaving behind a glass slipper. Hah. More like dawn and her knickers. Chastity was never one of her virtues.

When the dogs struggle to their feet and nose me with a whimper, I realize I've been moaning epithets out loud. I can no longer trust the *London Times*. Shouldn't a book reviewer check out the facts? Readers deserve the truth. Pick one: a hard-working mother, trying to teach responsibility, feed her family, and keep up a disintegrating castle? Or a surly borderline sucking all the air out the room?

By the way, aside from his eighty thousand acres, the Prince is no catch. He's a puffy-faced dissolute with bad teeth. And I hear he's tired of Ella's tantrums. He's sealed her into the tower and won't let her out until she agrees to therapy. She paces the ramparts in a frenzy, intermittently screaming. Or is that the peacocks I hear? From this distance, they sound the same.

Scritch

RONNIE'S BEEN RIDING his sister's bike for two hours in cold rain and has finally reached his destination, a house in the woods at the end of a long gravel driveway. He's wet, frozen, and numb and really wants to get inside this house. It's not much of a house, maybe four little rooms. Siding is rotten in places, gutters are rusting. He walks around it and looks in the windows. When he sees a woman in a lighted room, he pushes through prickly shrubbery to get closer, then stands on tip toe. Is she alone? There's no one else in the house as far as he can tell. The woman's name is Gloria and she doesn't resemble the pictures she sent him, where her hair was long and blonde. Now her hair's shorter, pulled back into a dinky tail except for what's falling in her face. She's older, too. Should he bother? What the fuck. He's here and she'll let him in, she was all hot to meet him in her letters.

His cell mate at Butner told him about PrisonPenPals, and though Ronnie didn't think women would write to a sex offender, right after his ad went on the Internet, he started getting letters with pictures and proposals for sex, love, or marriage. Since he never answered back, most of the pen pals gave up, but three of them kept on sending letters, every week for eight years. He kept their pictures taped to the wall next to his bunk. With her long blonde hair, Gloria was his favorite.

Ronnie's been out of Butner for a week. He's sleeping on his sister Kristy's sofa. The first day—Christ, the first hour—she shoved the newspaper at him and showed him a dishwashing job, seven bucks an hour plus a free meal. The free meal was why she wanted him to take the job. So that's how it's gone, her on his case about a plan, a job, starting out right, and he woke up this morning with a bad itch for a new and different relationship.

He knocks hard on Gloria's window and she jumps, then sees him. He's grinning hard as he can with his frozen face, just being friendly old Ronnie. He gets to the front door just as she does.

"Is it who I think it is?" says Gloria. She pushes her hair behind her ears and holds onto the door. He sticks out his hand until she takes it with limp fingers. He explains his early release, thanks her for writing and keeping him going all those years. Then she has to ask him in, just to be polite.

"You're so tall!" she says, not like her picture at all, where she looked like a model in high-heeled boots and a leather jacket. In person she's mousy, with bags under her eyes and a wrinkly neck.

"You got your hair cut," Ronnie says. "Looks nice." He wants to give her a little squeeze, but she keeps backing away. He's pissed that she's not more excited, that he's having to do all the work.

"Sit, please sit! I'll get us some tea." She backs into the kitchen and Ronnie sits, glad to be where it's warm even though he hates tea, it tastes like what you'd expect from dried leaves. He wants to change his order, get a beer instead, and gets up to follow her into the kitchen, where he sees she's picked up the phone and is dialing. 9-1-1? No, too many numbers.

"I was just going to call out for a pizza, how's that sound," Gloria says. "Pepperoni and mushroom?" She orders the pizza, gives her address, then the teakettle is whistling and she pours water into mugs. He doesn't want to be caught staring at her body but when she turns her back to pour the tea, he studies her, looking for curves under the baggy sweat shirt, feeling a rising tension like a zoo lion waiting for dinner. He'll have to be patient, make himself invisible when the pizza guy arrives.

Gloria is flushed and acts nervous, patting pillows and humming. "How's it feel to be out?" she asks. "What's the best part about being a free man?"

He laughs. The best part, which he isn't going to tell her, is the end of sex offender therapy group, two hours of listening to I-Was-Drunk Franklin and Bible-clutching I-Only-Did-It-A-Few-Times Sid lie about controlling their deviant urges while the furry social worker drones on about denial, the blame game, and cognitive distortions. Every day Ronnie had to come up with his own lies and apologetic speeches, such bullshit because he's nothing like these repulsives with their high-speed Internet and videos of Boy Scouts.

"Just being able to go where you want?" Gloria offers.

"That's it. I can wake up in the morning, decide to visit pretty Gloria, and here I am." He sips the dusty tea, then gets up to look at pictures on a bookcase, mostly school pictures of two kids, a boy and a girl. "These your kids?" he asks.

Both are light-haired with tight smiles like their mom's, hardly showing any teeth. Maybe their teeth are crooked. In fact, the girl's wearing braces. Those braces, that shiny beige hair—she looks familiar. He shivers from a sudden chill.

Gloria grabs the picture and turns it face down. "Ronnie, you look cold. You want a fire?"

So she doesn't want to share her family with him, well, screw her. It bothers him that he can't remember where he knows the girl from. She wasn't a pen pal, none of them had braces. No, it's the picture he remembers, the smile with the wired teeth. He thinks it's a high school graduation picture.

She opens the fireplace doors and pokes at the ashes. "We'll need wood. Want to help me get some from the shed?"

"Fetch the wood? What else, wash the dishes? Walk the dog?" He smiles to show he's joking but he's always hated chores, working off the endless list every woman he's ever known spent her livelong day composing for him.

Gloria shakes her head, smiling tightly. "It'll just take a minute. Then our pizza should be here."

Her nervousness is making him antsy, so he shrugs, he'll go, he wants to move around. They pull on their coats. It's stopped raining now, and Ronnie sees his breath cloud in the moonlight. He reaches out to the back of Gloria's neck and squeezes the warm muscle until she stops walking. Her breathing is shallow and rapid. A long-lost strength enters his body and he gives Gloria a push, gets her moving again.

The shed's a crude log cabin with no windows and at first it's hard to see, even with the flashlight she swings about and shines onto the wood pile. "There it is," she says. "Watch out for mice!" As he leans over to pick up a few sticks of wood, the light goes out.

"Wait here," she says, "I'll get another flashlight." And then she's gone. He realizes she's shut him in.

He makes his way to the door. It's locked. When he shakes the door, nothing moves. It's a serious lock, probably a dead bolt, What kind of weirdo puts a dead bolt on a nothing shed? He stands there, waiting. Minutes pass. He sits down on the floor and hugs his knees.

A sliver of moonlight slips under the door. His eyes adjust to make out shapes. Not much in here but wood, a small mountain of it. He hopes Gloria gets over her stupid prank soon. It's very cold on the floor so he gets up and moves around. His pants are still damp from the rainy bike ride and he starts to shiver. Something rustles near the woodpile. Mice, she'd said. Hope to Christ it's not a snake.

Is she calling the cops? So he surprised her, that's not a crime last time he looked. It's so freaking cold his feet are going numb. He pulls his hands up into his jacket and dances, shuffles, trying to keep warm.

"Ronnie." It's Gloria, whispering at the bottom of the door. "Are you cold?"

"What's going on?" He's going to be polite, at least until he's got a hand on her scrawny neck again.

"Did you recognize her?" Gloria's whispering makes his skin crawl. He knows who she means, the girl in the picture.

"Recognize who?" Then he begins to remember. The newspaper articles, the pictures of the three who died in the trailer fire. Neil, wearing a Padres sweatshirt and holding a beer. The two girls' pictures from yearbooks, since they had just graduated and started college.

DNA evidence got him on the sexual assault charges, but Ronnie swore to the jury that Neil started the fire. And the jury believed him, they had to—there was no proof. The proof burned up and got their pictures in the newspaper. Yes, he thinks as his heart starts to pound out of his chest, one of the girls had shiny beige hair and braces. What. The. Fuck.

His throat tightens and he can't speak but he must. "Gloria? Sweetheart?"

"I'm just waiting for the others," she whispers. Something rustles behind him, behind the musty dry wood.

He shoves his hands in his pockets and touches the cord. "The others?"

"The other mothers. They'll be here soon. Are you cold?"

"Well, yeah." He chokes out a laugh. "You gonna let me out? Let's have a talk. We have things to talk about." He's now shaking violently, dancing from foot to foot.

"Talk all you want. I'm just going to light my lantern here." The scritch of a match, then a yellow glow under the door.

He scuttles to the door and crouches to catch any bit of warmth from the lantern. He's worried about what she said, the other mothers. "What's going on?"

"Don't worry. It won't be long now." She pauses for a moment. "I used to pray for death, until we thought of this. What does a man like you pray for?"

"Right now, a key to the door." His teeth are chattering so hard he can barely get the words out. "They said I wasn't guilty. I did my time on the other."

"You had a good lawyer, Ronnie. But there was no doubt, really. Wait. They're here." As Gloria walks away with the lantern, the glow disappears. He hears the thunk of car doors closing, and then nothing for a long while. He thinks he's going to freeze to death. It's not a bad way to die, he's heard, you just get drowsy and fall asleep. He's not at the drowsy stage yet. He's still at the violent shivering stage, all his bones rattling as he stamps the floor.

He finds a shovel and whacks at the walls, the roof, looking for a weakness. The logs are fit solidly together. Someone spent way too much time building this goddam shed. He gets the shovel into a chink and leans on the handle. It snaps and he falls, smacking himself in the face with the splintered end of the broken handle. It smarts like hell and tears come to his eyes.

Then he hears the whispering again. "Ronnie? We're all here. It's Cheryl and Jackie, remember us?"

"Let me out. Please. Please." He'll beg. Women change their minds when you beg, when you humiliate yourself. "I'm really sorry!"

"We've waited eight years, Ronnie. That's eight years more than they got."

His nostrils fills with the stink of gasoline. He hears the women murmuring, like prayer.

Brown Jersey Cow

I'M STIRRING A pot of stew, wishing I had a bit of ham for flavor 'cause grits and carrots make a bland mix. Baby's pulling on my skirt, wanting some now now now. My girls be digging for potatoes though I told them there ain't nothing but stones out there. It's been hard, our first winter on this hill with nothing put up. We're eating corn grits three times a day, with a wormy turnip or dried apple for interest.

My cousin Jack sets hisself down on the stool and tugs on his boots. Jack and my Mam had the same grandpa. After my husband's accident (fishing, fell in, drowned 'cause he never learned to swim) the children and I had nowhere to go but the old home place. If you picture a falling-down shack hanging on the side of a hill, you correctly vision Pappy's bequest to his only two living descendants: Jack and me. We share a house and seven rocky acres. Jack's simple—can't read nor write—but fifteen years older'n me so I can't tell him nothing. Last week Jack got out of jail after six months for selling moonshine.

"Where are you going?" I ask him.

"To fetch a pail of water."

"We don't need no pail of water," I say. "The cistern's full after last night's rainstorm."

Lightning and thunder had went on for hours, terrifying Pig. Pig's still jumpy this morning when I take him the slop bucket. Pig'll eat anything you can imagine and some stuff you'd think weren't food at all—paper, hair, dirt. There's not much by way of tasty scraps for him these days.

"Cistern water's no good for brewing."

"Are you crazy? Did you learn nothing from jail time?"

"I won't sell it. I'll give it away this time. Trade."

"Trade for food, right?"

"Maryjane."

"What?" Can't he hear my stomach rumble?

"Marijuana, dummy. I need seeds, fertilizer. Trade shine for money and buy what I need to grow it. Fellow I know made twenty thousand selling weed."

"Your cell mate?" I am too famished to argue the obvious, that trading for money is selling. Besides, I know Jack. Big on talk, not so much on follow-through. I can't see him weeding no pot plot.

Jack looks out the window. His brow is creased like he's thinking. Unlikely.

"If you're needing something to do, Cat's hidden her kittens again," I tell him.

He snorts. "The girls'll find 'em." He picks up the pail and strolls off.

I been extra low since my brown Jersey cow disappeared. Last I saw, she were in the cowshed, munching on hay. Jack says she were stolen. Only the devil would steal a cow from a hungry family like mine. The children miss her sweet creamy milk. Baby's not gained a pound since he turned one years old, and you can count the girls' ribs through their undershirts. It's a race to see what comes first, the month of April or someone dying.

I lean on the sill and look out at the mud, daydreaming about my garden. I'll sow tomatoes, peppers, peas, and beans for puttin' up. Fill the cellar with sweet potatoes, beets, and carrots. In the fall, I'll plant my greens. We'll not be hungry *next* winter. What I couldn't do with a bit of money. If I had money I'd buy Leghorn pullets, they's good layers.

But Jack's wanting to go for water makes me suspicious, since his motto is *why do today what I can put off forever* and he applies it to every minute of his life except meals, naps, and taking a crap.

So I follow him up the hill, a good piece behind. The mist is heavy, dampening my arms and face. He's hiking at a good pace, not his usual amble. When he gets to the well, I crouch behind a stone wall and watch. He lifts the cover off the well, reaches in, and pulls out a brick. Takes out a cloth purse and pours silver dollars into a pile! Clink, clink, clink.

I *knew* he were up to something!

Only *one* way he got that money. He's sold my cow, while the girls shiver and starve in their rags. I think about that money and my brown Jersey's sweet creamy milk. I think about our supper—grits with a carrot. I think about Baby's little stick arms, and I jump over the wall, grab the brick, and lay it hard upside his head. He flies tail over teakettle down the hill.

It's believed he stumbled, broke his crown. That *were* a possibility, the grass *were* wet. Coming down the hill I myself slip, the coins jingling heavy in my pocket.

I soak brown paper in cider vinegar and wrap his head, but he never opens his eyes. He breathes his last at midday. The girls cry for Uncle Jack until I promise 'em biscuits for supper. Pig eats the paper.

In the afternoon I go to town and buy a brown Jersey cow. Get a good price 'cause I'm a widow, and there's money left over for sugar and flour and six Leghorn pullets. At supper I spread butter on our biscuits and pour milk gravy over the grits. Baby eats until he can't move. I swear the girls grow an inch on the spot. We all enjoy the feeling of a full belly. Nothing's better than sweet creamy milk from a brown Jersey cow.

Something to Tell Henry

TUGGING ON HER floppy hat, Ava steps off the bus into the baking oven that is Tampa in July. She walks past pastel-colored stucco walls softened by red hibiscus and spiny agave, the only sound the stuttering of sulfurous sprinklers. An armadillo enlarges its burrow under an azalea bush. She watches for a moment. It's something to tell her son Henry about. Is an armadillo a reptile? Does it lay eggs? He will know, or pretend to know. Though only seven, he likes to be an expert in everything scientific.

Ava is the nanny for Terry and Clara Wicker's three-year-old twin sons. She got the job two months ago through her sister Fran, whose husband works in Terry's bank. Ava prefers being a nanny to her previous job at a daycare, except for Clara's never-ending requests for favors—"Ava, would you mind . . ." folding the laundry, starting dinner, cleaning up after Sigmund? Sigmund, a large colorful parrot, has the run of the house, and deposits crusty cement-like blobs wherever he perches. But the pay is decent and she enjoys working with two boys instead of a dozen. Even though the twins are holy terrors with ten-second attention spans, Ava's already made a difference in their lives. For one thing, they're now potty-trained, mostly. Clara still puts diapers on them at bedtime, but the first thing each morning Ava removes those diapers and lets them run around in their shorts, no underpants, so they can easily access their little squirters when they have to go. Clara gave Ava a fifty-dollar tip for potty-training them. Now Ava is working on their language, which, until recently, has been nearly unintelligible twin-speak. She withholds treats until they pronounce words correctly. It's working, almost too well. Just yesterday Dylan said perfectly, "I want more cookies, please," shrieking it over and over until he was banished to the naughty seat.

The Wicker house is a peach-colored stucco mansion on the bay, with a red tile roof and a flagstone courtyard already, at eight-thirty in the morning, stunningly hot. Once inside, Ava pulls a sweater out of her tote bag; Clara keeps the thermostat on frigid. In the Florida room, Joe and Dylan sit slack-jawed and unmoving in front of the TV—the only time they are ever immobile while awake—still wearing their pajamas. Cute dark-haired boys, with thickly-lashed blue eyes, dimples, and a sprinkling of freckles, they need activity. Today it's too hot for the park but they can play in the sprinkler to work off energy. She can drag their wading pool under the pergola so they'll be shaded. She sends them upstairs to put on their bathing suits and goes back to the kitchen to fill a pitcher with cold water.

Ava halts in the kitchen doorway because Terry Wicker stands by the sink, dressed for work in his banker's navy suit and shined shoes, his thick sandy hair gelled into submission. His unsmiling face is a particular shade of red Ava knows well. Her ex had the same dark flush, a sign of high blood pressure, booze, and a temper. Ava tends to avoid Terry though he is polite enough.

"Look." He points through a window. A few feet from the seawall, black dorsal fins break the bright choppy water. Dolphins. A pod, Henry has told her. A pod of dolphins. One of them spouts a gust.

"Cool," Ava says, "my son's favorite animal," though she suspects Henry would adore Sigmund, who clings to his perch in the sunny corner muttering as he combs through his feathers. She wishes Henry could hear the bird talk. Sigmund sounds exactly like Clara, who's taught him "don't worry, be happy," "peace, brother," and other upbeat sayings in her lisping girlish voice.

Terry drapes his jacket and tie over a chair. "My boys like T-Rex. Anything that roars and bites and scares the crap out of people. Like them."

Ava laughs. "You're right. They're tough."

"We must've had hardy forefathers. Clara and I are easily bruised types." A smile opens his face, suddenly likeable. He goes out the back door into the garage. Through a kitchen window she sees him come around the corner wheeling a metal tank and carrying a long wand. He aims the wand at the ground and a blast of flames roars out. He sweeps it back and forth over the white gravel, incinerating every stray blade of green. Now that's something to tell Henry, how Mr. Wicker uses a flamethrower to get rid of crabgrass.

"Ava?" Clara calls from the top of the stairs. She wears a white negligee so sheer that Ava can see her dark nipples and bikini underpants. She is not a typical mother-of-toddlers like the daycare moms, frazzled-looking women who put themselves last, no makeup, hair scraped into a pony tail. Curvy and dimpled, with dark-gold hair flowing over her shoulders, Clara had been some sort of entertainer, a dancer or possibly a stripper, before getting pregnant with the twins and marrying Terry, a bank president. Marriage hasn't changed her clothing style—skin-tight with cleavage—though according to Fran the labels have had a significant upgrade. Fran says everyone at Terry's bank thinks Clara is a piece of work.

Clara tilts her head and bites her lower lip, a flirty look. "If you have time today? Terry loves your potato salad. And oven-fried chicken. And while the boys are sleeping, the living room needs cleaning." The living room needs cleaning because Sigmund frequently perches in there. It's easy to get his poop off the marble floors, swirled pink-white-brown like Neapolitan ice cream, but the blobs stick to the upholstery. "One other thing. Can you take the boys out this afternoon? I need privacy."

Ah. Ava studies Clara's face, her almond eyes, dark brows like crescent moons, slightly pink skin. Pink with guilt, perhaps. Ava strongly suspects that Clara wants them gone so that she can spend the afternoon with her lover. Ava's never met the man, but nearly every time she takes the boys out to give Clara "privacy," a black Ford 350 will be parked down the street, *Eric Nowicki, General Contractor* printed on its door. And once she overheard Clara on the phone, talking about Eric and his penis the size of a beer can. "A tall boy, not the twelve-ounce," she'd whispered, giggling. Something Ava would rather not know, though the image is now stuck in her head.

"It's kinda hot to be outside," Ava says.

"You can take my car. Go to the mall or the movies. I'll pay extra."

Ava shrugs. "Sure." The money is a bribe to buy her silence, completely unnecessary concerning the business with Eric since Ava wants no part of the Wicker family melodrama. She's happy to go to the mall and know nothing, la-la-la-la-la, avoid the man entirely.

"Try to be gone by one."

"The boys don't wake up until two."

"Then get them up early." Clara sounds exasperated.

Okay. Clara doesn't care how tired, cranky, and hyperactive her sons are, as long as they are out of the house when Eric arrives. Ava goes back to the kitchen muttering the words she saves up to say when no one is listening: *useless fucking whore*, repeating the words until she passes the dining room and realizes that Terry stands inside the doorway. He has come in from the yard. He has heard her. His bleak angry eyes bore into hers, and she looks right back, embarrassed. She smacks her hand over her mouth. "Geez, sorry."

"No problem." His expression is frozen but his face matches the dining room walls, tomato soup.

She feels an impulse to say more, to make an excuse for Clara, then an impulse to warn Clara that Terry might have heard her—competing impulses that cancel each other out.

AS POTATOES SIMMER and breaded chicken bakes, Ava watches the boys splash in the wading pool. She's lulled by a breeze warming her skin, the iodine smell of the sea, the cries of gulls. She wonders what her son is up to in his classroom. He doesn't seem to miss having a dad. Before Henry was born, his father lit out for Nevada to find work, promising to send money. Though she never heard from him again, Ava managed. She and Henry lived with Fran while Ava earned her associate's degree in early childhood, not a money-making career but Medicaid and food stamps kept them healthy and fed. She's even bought a little house recently, a fixer-upper near Fran's, and does that feel good, her own place with a yard. Not the greatest neighborhood, but a short walk to the bus, the library, the school.

A cry for help startles her. Leaving the boys fighting over the hose, Ava finds Clara in the courtyard, dancing around the base of a royal palm. Thirty feet above them, Sigmund nestles in the fronds, preening and muttering to himself.

"I'll get a ladder if you want," Ava says.

"No, he'll fly away. He'll only come down when he wants to. Problem is the other birds will attack him, he's so big and odd." Clara sighs. "Ava, dear, do you know what I need? I need a mud wrap. Get me an appointment for eleven, would you? The spa number's on the bulletin board. You'll keep an eye on Sigmund, won't you? Keep him out of trouble."

Add *parrot rescue* to Ava's list of chores.

AVA CALLS THE spa to make Clara's appointment. The receptionist is rude, inspiring thoughts about making numerous fake appointments. Maybe another day. Ava is horrified by the price—$195 would feed Henry and her for a month. Clara seems so careless with her money. Terry's money. Many of the clothes in Clara's over-stuffed closet still sport price tags, and there are at least sixty pairs of shoes. How many shoes do you need? Well, Ava needs another pair—her left big toe is starting to poke through—but it's not until the fourth paycheck each month that she has any extra cash. She's been saving up a cushion, a few hundred dollars so she won't have to worry about getting sick, or buying medicine. If they stay healthy, knock knock, some day she might be able to afford a car. Today's bonus will go to a new pair of shoes for herself, and a trip to the thrift store to buy pants for Henry.

She gives the boys lunch then drags them protesting into their beds where they immediately fall into a deep sleep. She boils eggs, chops celery, pickles and onions, and mixes it all together with the potatoes and lots of mayo. In the living room she sprays cleaner on the coffee table, a slab of glass on driftwood legs. A brick planter is crammed with fake dust-coated plants. More spray, more wiping. Sigmund has pooped all over the leather sofa so she mists the sofa liberally, leaving the cleaner to work. A shelf holds dozens of dusty glass figurines and she wipes them one by one, admiring a little dolphin in a graceful mid-leap.

Outside, Sigmund has migrated to the back of the house, high up in a clump of palm trees leaning over the seawall. She calls out to him, and the bird caws but doesn't budge. A pair of seagulls circles the clump of trees and lands close to him. "Peace!" he says, as one of the gulls opens its wings and hops toward him. Sigmund raises his crest, cries, "Peace!" again, and takes flight. The gulls attack him, screeching, diving until they knock Sigmund into the water. Ava watches to see if he can swim, but his feathers are soaked and he bobs up and down with the lapping waves. He looks stunned, his beady eyes closed. She trots onto the dock and grabs a fish net hanging from a hook. The water isn't very deep so she removes her shoes, climbs down the ladder, and wades over to Sigmund. She scoops him up in the net and cuddles him as he mutters little caws. She wonders if the swim will loosen his feathers. She has been wanting one for Henry, but Sigmund doesn't seem to shed.

AWAKENED TOO EARLY, the boys are cranky as hell as Ava jollies them into going potty then putting on their shoes. She has to promise ice cream to get them into the car. Clara's Cadillac is custom-painted a pale mint green and clean as new. Ava drives slowly. She likes driving a rich lady's Cadillac, pretending it is her car.

They wander around the mall for hours eating ice cream and candy, playing in the mall play space, riding the escalators. It's not hard to entertain three-year-olds if you devote yourself to them utterly, and that is Ava's job. At four o'clock, the boys have had enough of the mall, and Ava figures it is safe to take them home.

Driving home, she passes Chickadees, the daycare where she used to work in the two-year-old classroom. Do the potty dance, sing the alphabet, feed dollies. An exhausting, hard job, where the kidlets clung to her all day, banged on each other, screamed "no" and "mine" every other word. Nanny work is much easier.

THE SIGHT OF Eric Nowicki's big black pickup in the driveway surprises Ava. Her heart begins to pound a little faster.

She turns to hush the boys. Joe has just socked Dylan, who is shrieking like it doesn't happen twenty times an hour. Dylan reaches out and grabs Joe's ear and pulls, hard. Ava needs to get rid of these children, collect her paycheck, and catch the 5:12 bus in order to pick up Henry at Fran's by five-thirty. She refuses to drive around for another hour, waiting for Eric to leave. She releases the twins from their car seats and leads them along the side of the house to the back door.

The house is freezing cold as usual, and quiet. Clara must be upstairs. "Can we watch a show?" Joe asks, enunciating perfectly, and Ava smiles at him for being such a good little talker. TV will keep them quiet, occupied, while she figures out what to do. She turns on the TV and gives them a bowl of pretzels. With a table knife she begins to scrape the softened blobs from the leather sofa. They come off easily, and she is soon finished. Now what? She stands at the bottom of the stairs, listens, hears the murmur of their voices. Clara's bedroom door must be open. For Christ's sake, doesn't Clara realize the boys are here?

Ava climbs the stairs, leans against the wall, and knocks on the door frame. "Uh, Clara? I have to leave now."

Clara says, "Come on in, honey."

Ava doesn't move. "It's Friday and I need to get paid."

A man appears in the doorway, muscular and shirtless. His thickly-lashed blue eyes are wide-apart, his skin lightly freckled. Ava takes him in, the dark floppy hair, the deep dimples as he grins, and she gasps, not because he's nice-looking, not because he's half-naked in Clara's bedroom with a tall boy in his pants. She's shocked because she's seen the smaller versions of his face a thousand times in the past two months. She claps her hands to her mouth. Over Eric's shoulder she sees Clara reclining in bed, smiling at her, her head tilted. Repulsive.

"What the fuck is going on?" Ava asks. Clearly it's not necessary to be polite.

Eric takes hold of Ava's arm with a vise-like grip, locking her gaze until she flushes and sweat breaks out on her face. "You gonna tell on us?"

She yanks out of his grasp. "I need to get paid."

"Can it wait till Monday?" Clara asks in her whispery voice from inside the bedroom.

"No." Ava doesn't feel like explaining that she has to buy groceries, pay the electric bill.

"Bring me my checkbook then, in my purse. Downstairs."

She finds Clara's purse, a beautiful red Coach bag, and rummages for the checkbook. She glances at the twins; they are feeding each other pretzels as Ernie sings about his rubber ducky.

Upstairs again, Clara's wrapped the sheet around her chest, dark-gold hair tangled on her bare shoulders. Eric sits on the bed, tying his shoes. The room smells of perfume and sweat. "Shouldn't he be hiding in the closet?" Ava's voice is strangled, she can barely choke out the words.

Flushing, Clara hands her a check. "There's extra for you." She's added a hundred to Ava's weekly wage.

"It's not right, you know. The boys might come up here."

"Well, they didn't, did they?"

"Terry will be home any minute."

Clara sinks down onto her pillow, turns onto her side, pulls the sheets over her shoulders. "You better say nothing. And go."

"That's right." When Ava shuts the bedroom door, she is shaking. What a mess.

AVA UNZIPS THE red Coach bag, takes out Clara's wallet with its wad of cash, and removes six twenties. *Clara will never miss it, she doesn't know what she has.* She goes into the living room and slips the glass dolphin into her pocket. She scoops half the potato salad into a plastic tub along with four pieces of the oven-baked chicken and puts the container into her tote bag, along with a bottle of citrusy bath gel, part of a gift set Clara's forgotten about in the laundry room.

She kisses the boys' freckled noses, forcing Joe then Dylan to meet her gaze for an instant with their lovely blue eyes.

"Goodbye, little friends," she says, and they turn back to the TV. Elmo is talking about imagination, something Ava needs no more of today.

As she's smartly plucking a green feather from Sigmund's tail—he doesn't say a word—she hears the garage door open. It's Terry, no doubt rolling his gold Lexus past Eric's black pickup. *This is going to be interesting* but Ava won't stay to witness Terry's humiliation. She folds her sweater and tucks it in her tote bag. She opens the back door, stands aside to let Terry in. He's even more red than usual.

"Why is that prick here?" he asks.

Ava shrugs. "I have to leave now. The boys are watching TV." She studies his face. Is he angry? Perhaps ashamed that there's a witness. "I won't tell anyone," she says. He nods, then charges past her, knocking a stool to the floor. She pictures Eric burned black and crispy by the flamethrower.

The twins will be okay, she hopes, though Sesame Street will never produce the Big Bird episode addressing this particular muddle.

AT FRAN'S, HENRY sits on the steps clutching his backpack. He jumps up. "Look, Mom, I got a WOW sticker. I was the only kid in the class to get one today. Mrs. Harmon says I am a whiz at math, and I am way ahead on my book tally, I've read sixteen books this month. Knock, knock." He waits. "I said, knock, knock, Mom." His hair is sweaty, his glasses smudged, and something sticky has spilled down his front and collected grime. They walk along slowly, three blocks to their house.

Ava's been murmuring oh my, and that's great. "Sorry, who's there?"

"Mister."

"Mister who?" She takes Henry's hand and squeezes it.

"Sorry I missed her name, what is it again?"

"You're funny." Ava unlocks the door to her frame house with its four cramped rooms and peeling paint. She wants to scrape and paint it soon. She has almost decided on yellow but might go with a light creamy green like the Cadillac. She puts out the chicken and potato salad, glad she doesn't have to cook dinner.

Tucking Henry into bed, Ava gives him Sigmund's bright green feather, tells him about the parrot's escape and rescue. She sets the glass dolphin on his bedside table. "I saw a pod today."

"It's a bottlenose. They're the smartest of all dolphins," Henry says.

"I am the mother of the smartest dolphin."

"Where'd you get it?"

"Mrs. Wicker gave it to me." Ava slides Henry's glasses off his face and gently rubs the faint red marks they've left on each side of his nose. "Oh, and I saw an armadillo digging a burrow. Do they lay eggs?"

"Mom, it's so cool. They lay one egg, with four babies in it."

"Quadruplets."

"What's that?"

"Quadruplets, means four babies born at once."

"Your job is good, isn't it."

"Yes, sweetie. It's pretty good." Ava hugs her son for a long moment, pressing her face against his cool silky cheek. He smells faintly orange from the bath gel.

Ava counts her money. Forget new shoes, she'll need it all to tide her over while she finds a new job. Maybe a classrooms of fours. Fours use their words, love silly jokes. She can teach them letters, how to use scissors, the difference between right and wrong.

She lies down on her bed, feeling wiped out. She thinks about Terry's face when he'd overheard her call Clara such a terrible name. Did he already know about Eric? Had he seen the truck parked outside his house all those afternoons? Did he know *everything*?

She allows herself a brief pang of sadness at having to leave the boys. Goodbye, little friends. Hang tough.

The Fitting Room

GOOD MORNING! WELCOME to Bridal Boutique. *You ignored our discreet sign: by appointment only? You are six bored women with nothing better to do. Why me, oh lord?*

I'm Julie, and I'll be your consultant today. Which of you is the blushing bride? *Why are they looking at each other, don't they know? Oh no, that one, I was afraid it would be her. Clutching her Happy Meal.*

Well, this is an exciting day, isn't it! The day you find the perfect dress. And your name is . . . ? *Dayton. I'm terrible with names. Think of Daytona Beach, where I wasted many a weekend working on my tan and am now paying the wrinkly price.*

Dayton, when's the big date? *Better be soon, you are showing already. Four months along, I'd guess. You shorter girls poke out early.*

Oh my, that doesn't give you much time. Well, we better get busy then, hadn't we? *You have got to be kidding. What kind of girl walks in here needing a dress in two weeks?*

Who did you bring along today? I just love a cheering section! *Yeah, right, makes my job absolutely impossible. I have to please a seventeen-year-old pregnant bride, her mother, her future mother-in-law, her sister, and two girlfriends. My eyeballs are throbbing.*

Come along and we'll get settled into a fitting room. Can I get anyone something to drink? *Please say no, please say no. I hate drinks in the fitting room. They are always getting spilled.*

So that's three diet Cokes, a root beer, and two Cheerwines? Be right back. While I'm gone, would you fill in this questionnaire? *You* can *read and write, can't you, Dayton?*

Here you go. There are drink holders in the chairs. *Yes, it's just like the movies. Sit back and enjoy the show.*

Oh my, that's a bright flash! No cameras please. *Text and tweet all you want. Just no pictures of Dayton in her underwear on Instagram. If I gritted my teeth any harder they'd fracture.*

Looking at your answers, Dayton, I see that you are a size eight? *Maybe two years ago, before puberty hit you like a freight train.*

Our dresses run quite small, so we may have to go up a size or two. But you'll get a perfect fit, not to worry. Oh, you brought pictures? Very helpful. *Except these are Vera Wang. You're in the wrong salon, honey.*

And strapless? *No strapless dress was ever made that could cantilever those double-D girls.*

A long, full skirt? Shantung taffeta, beautiful choice. *You'll look like a giant marshmallow, child.*

I'm thinking an empire waist would suit you well. *Since you no longer have a real waist.*

And I'll try to stay in your price range, hmmm? *You've got to be kidding. Only our garters are in that price range.*

Be back in a minute. And while you wait, here are some style books. *No, I don't have six style books, you'll have to share.*

(Mutters to self as she searches through the dresses. *Empire waist, strapless, cheap, taffeta. Zilch. Okay, Plan B.*)

Well, Dayton, I found a dozen dresses and one is bound to be absolutely right. *Half of these are trampy and half are classy. Let's see, which will you like?*

Here comes the exciting part. Try this one on! Oops, let me hold the Coke. *It's very difficult to get Coke out of silk.*

Hmmm. What do you think? *I think it makes you look like a manatee in a ball gown.*

Let's try another one. This ivory is beautiful with your skin. *I'd kill for your skin, not a pore to be seen.*

Too low cut? Possibly. *No one will be able to focus on the ceremony for fear of the reveal.*

Maybe one with a slightly narrower skirt? To give you a more vertical look? *Did I actually say that? Hope she doesn't realize that vertical is the opposite of wi-i-i-i-ide.*

Very nice. Oh, mom doesn't like the pearl beading. *Mom, shut up.*

What do you think of this—no beads, sweet neckline, an A-line skirt? *Ignore your sister. She's not on your side.*

Well, it will be your very special day and you are worth every penny. *Of course it's too expensive.*

If you want my opinion, I think a bit of sleeve would be very flattering. *If ever* anyone *needed straps. Wide and sturdy.*

Mom agrees? And Mumsie? Great! So let me get a few more. I'll be right back. *I am starting to sweat.*

Here we are. I just know THE DRESS is one of these. *Oh lord, there goes the root beer. Fortunately it's only saturating our pink plush carpet, not the pleated charmeuse.*

Don't worry about that. Here, I'll just get a towel. *I'm going away now, for ten minutes, to sullenly smoke a cigarette and wonder when and where my life took this turn, and if it's too late to go back there.*

I'm back! How's it going? Any luck? She *looks happy but no one else does. Does that mean . . . YES!*

Your son will think it's too plain? *We could appliqué sequined red roses all over it, Mumsie, if that would make you happy. Oops, I forgot, we don't care what* you *think.*

I'm so glad I was able to help. Leave it for a week to be shortened. *And don't gain more than five pounds.*

Thank *you,* Dayton, it was a great pleasure. *I can't believe she hugged me. Doesn't anyone respect boundaries anymore?*

Oh! I didn't realize *all* of you needed dresses. Okay, ladies, fill out these questionnaires. *Remarkable how the promise of a* big *commission check does wonders for a headache.*

Can I get anyone another soda?

Bullet Proof

HER BROTHER, A gang outreach worker in Durham, told Lisa about the job. He said a drug interdiction unit was looking for women to work with the police to entrap drug dealers, street sellers. It sounded easy—drive around on the weekends and buy drugs—and Lisa could sure use the paycheck. Plus, she hated drug dealers. Her dead husband had been an addict and never could stay clean what with the dealers crawling over him.

She worked the drug stings in Durham for a few months, then began to get calls from drug cops in small towns all over the state. From the start, the stings felt like God's work for her, and she was good at it. Every weekend, a new neighborhood, eight-nine junky sellers nailed. Like picking ticks off a dog. Though the next day there'd be new ticks, it was satisfying to temporarily clean up the dog, get the little buggers and flush them. The work was a welcome change from the nursing home. Not to mention, she was off her feet.

She felt uneasy leaving her children for the long weekend day, though neither Adam nor Emily seemed to care. Adam had his video games, his friends on the block, his bike for getting around. Eighteen-year-old Emily slept until noon, and then spent two hours talking on the phone, drying her hair, getting ready to go out. If Lisa asked where, Emily would shrug and smile patiently, flashing her dimples at her pathetic mom with no sex life. Someone would pick her up, and she'd be gone until three or four in the morning. If Lisa had behaved that way, her father would have slapped her in the face and locked her in her room for a month. But Emily had no father, just a mother who loved her, would never hit her, knew she was smart and wanted something better for her. Lisa had watched in confused despair as her daughter took up with a Marine Corps private, a waiter, and, one right after another, three players on the local college's soccer team. The soccer players were perpetually hungry, devouring scrambled egg-and-cheese burritos before thanking Lisa politely and disappearing with her daughter for the rest of the night.

When Emily's tastes in men changed to older, married ones, Lisa didn't know whether to feel better or not. At least a married man might have someone to turn to when Emily tired of him. The waiter had stalked her daughter for months, peering in their windows and calling so often that Lisa had to change their cell carrier, a two-hundred dollar penalty for canceling the contract.

Then Lisa heard rumors about an insurance salesman. When his wife found out he'd been sleeping with Emily, she left him, took their four kids to Florida and filed for divorce. Lisa didn't understand how Emily could be so unaffected by the damage she caused. "What was so irresistible?" Lisa asked. "Were you in love with him?"

"God, no." Emily was in a meditative mood, rocking on the porch, smoking a cigarette. She'd kicked off her sandals, her feet rested on the dog. "He was cute, don't you think? But desperate." She smiled, and Lisa felt an urge to slap that sly smirk hard, like her father would've done.

"Can't you date someone single? You're screwing up people's lives."

"Single guys are too easy. I like a challenge."

What did she mean, a challenge? Like that old song, whatever Emily wants, Emily gets. Emily was rudely beautiful, with a tick-tock walk that slowed traffic. She'd wink at a man, saying "I know what you're thinking" and she was usually right. She ignored her mother's warnings and cautions. She was bullet proof.

LISA SOON HAD her favorite cop, Sergeant Sterling. He wasn't good looking, with reddish thinning hair and a weak chin, but more fit than you'd expect of someone who spent all day in a patrol car. He was going to law school at night. Lisa trusted him. She wanted Emily to meet him, because she thought Emily would recognize his fine qualities. He was a man with moral strength who could lead a family, not slap them into obedience. If Emily was so determined that men were her calling, Lisa would show her a better class of man.

So, the next time Sergeant Sterling called her to work a sting he was setting up, Lisa asked him if Emily could be her partner. He asked how old Emily was, and when she told him eighteen, Sergeant Sterling hesitated only a second before saying, sure. A few weeks later, on a hot Saturday morning in May, she and Emily drove to Tyler, an hour from their home in Roanoke Rapids. Emily slept the entire way.

They met Sergeant Sterling at a church, where he would monitor them on the one-way voice link from their car. He was a serious cop, meticulous about protocol and paperwork. He called them Miss and Mrs. Castilla, and his gaze never dropped below their chins, even though anyone could see Emily's nipples through her white tank top that said "Martini Chick" and showed a good four inches of silky flat tummy down to low-rise jeans. He gave them the plastic bags for storing the product as they received it, and reviewed how to seal and sign the bag, then bring it back to the church where he'd be waiting. He went over procedures, how they should never get out of the car. How, for each buy, one of them would be the designated buyer, and the camera should be aimed at her window, to capture the transaction.

With the policewoman acting as a dealer, they did a trial run in the church parking lot, testing the camera and the voice link. During this rehearsal, Lisa saw Emily was sulking, because no one was entranced by her tank top, and she obviously didn't think Sergeant Sterling was cute. In Lisa's opinion, cute and $1.39 would get you a Slurpee. She hoped Emily would change her mind once they'd made a few buys and ID'd the sellers in Sergeant Sterling's photo albums. See that it was interesting, useful work.

Lisa pulled out of the church parking lot, turned right on Tenth Street, and slowed to a crawl. She scanned the houses as they rolled by, looking for a sign that neglect and decay weren't the only forces at work inside the concrete block houses with their yards full of weeds and trash. By a yellow-painted door, a child in diapers scratched in the dust. He raised a stick and pointed it at them like a gun.

Although she'd never been on these streets before, Lisa knew this neighborhood—she'd grown up in one exactly like it. She knew plenty of addicts, too, and didn't fear them. Addicts were after one thing—their next fix. They broke in and stole from your pocketbook and they sold themselves to get money to get high. If you had good strong locks on your doors and windows and didn't carry a pocketbook they'd look for easier prey. No, she didn't fear them. As she'd told Emily and Adam, they were a waste of skin.

Inevitable as a roach, here came the first crackhead, a white woman perhaps thirty, almost pretty, with a pixie face and clean brown hair in a ponytail. Lisa rolled down her window and asked the woman for a twenty. The woman leaned down and looked them over. Ignoring the whole business, Emily got out a cigarette.

"Sure. Circle around and come back in ten minutes," the woman said. Not so pretty after all—some teeth were missing.

Lisa circled, down Twelfth Street, left on King, left on Tenth, slowing down as she turned onto Harrison. The camera ran all the time, aimed at Lisa's window, filming trees and power lines and the four-way stop sign.

Emily pushed in the car lighter. It didn't work. "Got a match?"

"No, sorry."

Emily said she was bored, she couldn't breathe, and rolled down her window. "Mom, you shouldn't wear capris, with your legs."

Long ago, Lisa had developed an immunity to her daughter's insults. "It's my disguise today. I'm a fat lady with no fashion sense."

"No, I mean you look OK in jeans. But not capris." Emily tapped the cigarette on her leg. "I need a light."

"Maybe that woman has a lighter. They usually do."

"How can you do this? Ride around pretending to be an addict?"

"It gets them arrested, off the street."

"You do it for the money."

"No, for the adventure."

"You're kidding. This is the most boring day of my life."

Sergeant Sterling was listening and Lisa felt embarrassed. She touched her daughter's arm and pointed to the camera. "Look,

what we say is being recorded. It might get played back in court."
She would make a few more buys and then take Emily home.

Lisa's phone rang. Adam. She stopped the car to take her
son's call; he wanted to ride his bike to Walmart. Answering that
particular call turned out to be a mistake because while she was
insisting to Adam that no, he must not under any circumstance
go to Walmart, Emily opened the car door and got out. Lisa
snapped her phone shut and leaned across the seat. "What are
you doing?"

"I need a light."

"We'll get you a light. Get back in the car."

"I can't do this today. It's dirty."

The drugs were dirty, yes. Lisa carried baby-wipes to clean
her hands after handling them. But that's not what Emily meant.
"What's dirty about it?"

"You're lying to them. It's like cheating."

"You're one to talk about cheating."

Emily slammed the car door. "OK. I'm done."

"Get back in the car." Without a shred of authority. Lisa knew
she had lost.

"I'll be at the church." Emily walked away, back up Harrison
toward Tenth.

Sergeant Sterling would've heard this exchange through the
voice link, and he'd expect to see Emily in a few minutes. She
decided to circle once more, complete the buy, return to the
church, pick up Emily, and go home. This day was an experiment
that had failed.

The buy went smoothly, but when Lisa returned to the church,
Emily wasn't there. Sergeant Sterling took the labeled bag, made
a note of its weight and the time. "I think you look pretty good
in capris," he said.

Lisa laughed, embarrassed, ashamed of Emily's back talk,
Emily's behavior.

"Want me to help you find your daughter?" he asked.

"Gosh, no," Lisa said. "I know where she is. Don't want to
trouble you." He didn't seem surprised when she said she was
done for the day.

"I'll give you a call the next time," he said. She didn't think he'd ask her again. The sting was ruined, she was undependable.

Lisa drove around fruitlessly for an hour, increasingly alarmed, searching for Emily but seeing only seedy men and skanky women who waved and nodded, encouraging her to stop and buy. Her gut cramped with worry. Emily's cell phone lay on the car seat, useless.

Finally she parked where she'd last seen Emily. She hunched over her knotted stomach and waited. A young kid approached, already addict-yellow under his tattoos, sixteen going on sixty, smelling sour like vomit. He asked what she wanted and Lisa described her daughter. The kid had seen her. "Yeah, she's with Moon," he said.

"Moon?"

He pointed to a gray cinder block house. "I'll show you." Lisa got out of the car and followed.

Beer cans and shreds of Styrofoam littered the crabgrass. The two of them climbed concrete steps to a small porch, stepped over a flat of shriveled marigolds. Ignoring the doorbell in a corona of grime, the kid pushed the door open and they entered a room with three plastic chairs and a plasma TV. The carpet was black with dirt, worn away to the subfloor in places, speckled with what looked like lumps of dog shit. The kid pointed to a chair and Lisa perched gingerly on the edge. He walked part-way down a hall and yelled, "Moon! Moon!" A pacifier lay on the floor. What pathetic excuse for a mother would bring a baby here?

If Lisa had been alone, she would've hopped around the dried dog turds and skedaddled right out the dirty door, into her car, down the street to King Boulevard, home to Roanoke Rapids. But she couldn't leave Emily in the company of these dopers. She decided to follow the tattooed kid down the hall. He pushed open a door. Lisa stood on tiptoe and looked over his shoulder.

"Hey, Mom!" Emily grinned. "How'd you find me?" She lounged on a stained mattress. The man lying next to her squeezed her thigh. He was big, fine, and clean, in a white shirt and dark pants like a businessman, too good-looking for this revolting house. They both were. They beamed at Lisa as though pleased to see her. Moon had beautiful white teeth. "Welcome, madam," he said. His voice was rich, Jamaican.

Lisa tried to breathe. "What are you doing?" She pushed the tattooed kid aside. "Come on, honey. Let's go." She gently tugged on Emily's arm but the girl pulled back.

"Mom, chill!" Emily patted the mattress. "Have a seat."

"I'm taking care of her, Mom, don't worry," Moon said. He slipped his fingers under the strap of Emily's tank top. Lisa slapped his hand away and hauled hard, pulling her daughter up. Emily winked at Moon. "See ya," she said, and allowed Lisa to lead her out of the house.

It wasn't until Lisa made Emily fasten her seat belt that she noticed the glass pipe in Emily's hand.

LISA STILL CHEWS on that day. What kind of mother cruises around nodding at addicts, pretending to be one of them? Takes a daughter to a crap neighborhood to meet a dreary future?

EMILY TOOK TO crack like it was her destiny. The years went by in a blur. Thefts, arrests, pregnancies, rehab. Recently, a months-long court process finally granted Lisa permanent custody of Emily's two children. Cecie's three, distractible, with the attention span of a fruit fly, but there's one idea she holds onto with a death grip. "Mommy come?" she asks, over and over. Lisa used to answer, "On the weekend, honey," but there is such sadness when Mommy doesn't come that Lisa now says she doesn't know. Six-year-old Jon doesn't ask, but when Emily stops by Lisa's house he watches her carefully. He looks to see who's driving the car, and tells his grandmother when Emily takes money from her pocketbook. When Emily leaves, Cecie mashes her face against the window and cries inconsolably. Jon shakes his head, his face hard as stone. "Stupid baby," he says.

SORTING SOCKS, FOLDING tee-shirts, Lisa turns on the radio to find a distraction from her thoughts. National Public Radio, something uplifting. She hears a charmingly-accented baritone describe *the luminous mystery of existence*, urging her to *reconnect with your hopes and dreams*. She shoves the laundry basket aside and turns up the volume. The words, that voice, mesmerize her. She wants more. At the end of the program, she hears the speaker's name, Deepak Chopra. The next day she goes to the library and checks out every book of his that she can find.

She puts *Quantum Healing* in her pocketbook for reading on her break. She forks over $123 to Barnes & Noble for the complete set of *Synchrodestiny* CDs. *Grow Younger, Live Longer* is on the floor by her bed.

During the day, Lisa is too busy to orchestrate her spiritual growth. The alarm goes off at six, starting the routine that gets her grandchildren ready for school and daycare. She drops Jon off at school, then takes Cecie with her to the Learning Tree Child Development Center where she wipes snotty noses and changes diapers for eight mind-erasing hours. Then she picks Jon up, runs an errand or two, and fixes one of the three meals the kids will eat: spaghetti, hot dogs, or mac and cheese. She lets them watch TV until Cecie bites Jon, or Jon punches his sister. Cecie bites without warning or cause, and it's a problem; at daycare several parents have complained about bite marks on their kids.

The children are calmed by a bath and stories. They finally sleep. In the blessed quiet, she emails Adam, homesick and suffering through Marine Corps boot camp. She calls Emily and leaves a message: *call me, hope you're well.* She still pays Emily's cell phone bill but hasn't had even a text in weeks.

Duty behind her, Lisa takes up her book. For two precious hours she struggles to keep her eyes open. Though Chopra doesn't seem to address her particular situation, his words are soothing and optimistic. *Seek balance. Find your inner voice amidst the silence. Breathe deeply, still your mind.* She'd like to still her mind, especially the part that revisits the image of how Emily looked last time, her face and arms scabby where she'd been digging at imaginary bugs. *Any aspect of reality can be changed at the quantum level by shifting its information and energy.* Surely an answer can be found somewhere in these enchanting passages about taking responsibility and sharing feelings and moving on. *Find peace. Discover what really matters.* Nothing is changed, nothing will change, but the words dissolve her cloud of misery, her eyes droop, and she falls asleep, still gripping the book.

SASE

HEADACHY, CONSTIPATED, AND guilt-ridden: a morning like every other. On the table, a ragged stack of paper: early drafts, comments from beta reader, vacation ideas folder (as if), bills awaiting payment. The cat is napping next to the dead printer. Dead. The writer is a deadbeat parent, at a dead end, brain in deadlock, approaching deadline.

The writer needs a break and browses Facebook. Reheats cold coffee. Picks nose, stares at screen. Cannot go on like this. Nevermore, quoth the raven, but how to quit? According to lawyer, the writer cannot quit: child support, IRS, contract, lawsuit. Over-priced lawyer. *How does he justify $285 an hour?* Loathes lawyer. Feels used. Loathes publisher, agent, editor, ex-spouse. Each wants a piece but pie plate is empty. Wants to be happy. *What would make me happy?* Easy. The writer envisions a stone cottage on the coast of Maine, cat dozing by blazing fire, a plate of fried trout, champagne. Weight of obligations has crushed the writer's spirit and creativity but not will. The writer Googles "arsenic."

THE FAMOUS LITERARY agent awakens to synchronized ice picks jabbing into her skull. Her mouth is full of old carpet and her guts are tremulous like Jell-O. She screws her eyes shut but the skull stabs and internal quivering don't stop so she creeps to the bathroom for a BC powder, her favorite hangover treatment. There, top shelf, one envelope left. She drops it into water and sips the fizzy concoction slowly. She gags a little but it stays down.

I will never have another drink as long as I live. She can't remember the last time she felt this sick; forty-five is too old to chug White Russians. It was a fun boozy evening with her ex-husband, still her best friend. She divorced him after he confessed his penchant for dressing in chiffon, heels, and lipstick—and dating men—but he was still the most fun ever. They drank Pernod over ice at his apartment, then Rob Roys and Cab with dinner; so far so good, all under control, until the drinks at the club where her ex-husband's new friend Stan was performing. She isn't a music critic, but she formed an opinion of the new friend anyway—too much vamping and attitude to cover up his off-key crooning. Nonetheless she and her ex-husband applauded enthusiastically, and after his set, Stan joined them. He was an electric jazzy guy, a writer of gay sci fi erotica, and she remembers laughing too much at his stories. Her ex-husband ordered them all White Russians. The drink was delicious, like coffee ice cream. She ordered another one, and perhaps a third. She doesn't remember the trip back to her apartment. Her ex-husband must have put her in a cab.

The BC powder does its work and she begins to feel better. She makes coffee and takes a mug into the far end of her living room, stopping to feed the tank of betas. They dart to the top as she drops in a pinch of fish food. Snails have taken over the tank and it needs cleaning, but she can't abide the smell of it. It will wait until tomorrow.

Along the wall is the Pile; a stack of thousands of query letters and manuscripts. Each day's mail brings fifty letters or so, almost twice as many as she can process on a good day. Which today is not.

Two hours later the famous literary agent has made her way through seventeen envelopes. She has stuffed and licked fifteen SASEs, thirteen with form rejection letters and two with a request for a partial. Two queries didn't include a SASE—those she throws away.

At noon she gets dressed and leaves the apartment. She has projects to pitch to a senior fiction editor from The Press over lunch. She'll just have a salad because she still feels queasy. *And no alcohol.*

The famous literary agent makes it as far as the mail box. As she slips the letters into the slot, she's gripped by a sharp cramp in her gut. Her legs turn to jelly, the world spins, and she collapses to the sidewalk. A pimply kid in baggy jeans and a Mets ball cap leans over her. "You OK?" She moans, helpless, as he slides her wallet out of her purse and jogs down the street. She's never had a hangover this bad. *I am never going to drink again.*

And she never does.

THE SENIOR FICTION editor of The Press removes the lid from the purple box containing *Magical Fire*, Quincy Quaid's latest manuscript, its pages emitting the faint bug spray fumes of the author's perfume. For the past thirteen years it has been the senior fiction editor's job to turn Quincy's sludgy prose into readable books. She knows what she'll find: untethered participles, extraneous talky characters, confusing POV shifts. She scans page one. The word "actually" leaps out at her. She actually, really hates that word. She makes a purple dot in the margin.

Quincy Quaid's books are virtual heaving seas of emotion: longing, despair, lust, pain, humiliation, joy. Writing-wise, Quincy has slacked off in recent years, each new manuscript a half-ream of clichéd descriptions, flat characters, and unresolved plot threads. Whole passages are copied from earlier books, as though her readers won't remember. But of course they will; they are eagle-eyed spotters of lazy writing and sloppy editing. Obsessed fans have created Quincy Quaid websites where they post the mistakes and errors the senior fiction editor has overlooked, relatively few for over a hundred books but nonetheless embarrassing.

The senior fiction editor sighs and looks at her watch. Thirty minutes to lunch; enough time to reject a batch of queries, a mindless activity that will give her the illusion that she is, actually, working. She pushes aside the purple box and starts opening envelopes. By noon, three dozen SASEs are stuffed with a photocopied rejection letter, licked, sealed, and dropped into the mail slot. She sets aside the non-fiction queries to give to her boss, the publisher of The Press (and ex-husband of a famous literary agent) and then wanders down the hall to the break room. Some generous soul has sent a gift box of fruit. She selects a pear and bites into it. Crisp, juicy, an almost citrusy flavor. Very good.

Feeling refreshed, the senior fiction editor pours herself a cup of decaf and walks back to her office to tackle *Magical Fire*. She sits down and picks up the purple felt-tip pen. The first time through she always reads for story, making dots in the margin as errors catch her attention. Dot, dot, dot. Rachelle, an innkeeper, encounters Damon, a sexy brooding ghost who time-transports her to his Wales castle and the year 833. The senior fiction editor scans Chapter 2 several times; something is missing. Rachelle zips back to the ninth century whenever Damon summons her. But why does Damon pick *her*, out of all the women available to him throughout the span of human history? Oh God, this is going to be a real slog. She feels a little nauseous. Nine more years until retirement, she thinks. Maybe earlier if I cut back, move somewhere cheaper, someplace warm. Lower taxes. She turns on her computer and begins to search real estate prices in Raleigh. Suddenly, saliva fills her mouth and she retches. A godawful cramp seizes her gut and she feels faint and clammy. Quite ill, then even worse, actually.

THE PUBLISHER SLIDES his feet into the pair of red Marabou slip-ons, women's size fourteen, that he keeps hidden under his desk. He waggles his toes, feeling the feathers brush against his instep. The shoes calm him. They are a source of solace in difficult times, a bit of contentment. He isn't hung over, exactly, just exhausted; after they left the club last night, and he sent his ex-wife home, he spent the rest of the night trying to appease his new friend Stan, the club performer, who was turning out to be a jealous control freak, threatening suicide if the publisher doesn't end it with his ex-wife for good. The publisher's sour love life is a perfect book-end to the seemingly inevitable demise of The Press, sinking like the Titanic punctured by an iceberg of relentlessly bad sales.

Is it time to find a therapist, someone to listen empathetically? A therapist might be able to help him prioritize, give him some action verbs, such as "vanish." Jumping from a cruise ship might be easy to fake; they hardly ever recover the body, do they? He could buy a balcony room on a ten-day cruise, drink mai tais for a week, and then disappear. Leave a note in case no one notices he's missing, then hide out in the life boats or under a buffet table; there must be lots of good hiding places on those twelve-story floating cities. Stroll off the ship in Cozumel and never look back.

He gingerly rolls his head from left to right, bothered by a persistent ache in his neck. He tries to focus on the quarterly sales report. The Press's historical romance titles only broke even; it's impossible to compete with Harlequin, Random and Penguin in that category. Erotic did better; smutty sells. Quincy Quaid's revenues were a bit down, he notices, swallowing hard. If it weren't for her four books a year, The Press would have closed down years ago. Problem is, Quincy's advances deplete their capital, and where once he could borrow to keep the business running, now the banks act like every day is Sunday. If banks quit loaning money, how do they keep their buildings heated and all those vice-presidents paid? Oh, that's right—lifeblood-sucking extortionate credit card fees. The Cozumel cruise could go onto his Master Card, hee hee, soak up the last dollar of his credit limit.

Sighing deeply, the publisher speed-dials his ex-wife. He'll have to meet with her (without telling his new friend Stan) and renegotiate Quincy's contract. No one answers, so he leaves a message.

He picks up a handful of non-fiction query letters. The Press has a psychology "how-to" imprint, mostly books about codependency, of the "women-who-love-(fill in the blank)" variety. They published a blockbuster five years ago when sex addiction became such a, ahem, hot topic, and since then the publisher has read the best non-fiction queries, looking for the next big book. Alas, none of these is it. He slips a standard rejection into each of the SASEs and seals them.

His stomach growls. He never eats breakfast. It's a waste of good calories, better used on something tasty, something to lift his mood, like chocolate or smoked salmon. He takes off the slippers and walks down the hall to the break room for some coffee. He sees the pears but the publisher avoids fruit unless it's baked in a pie. He pours himself a cup of coffee, adds cream and takes a sip; it tastes metallic and he feels a bit shivery all of a sudden. Then dizziness tips his world sideways and clobbers him to the gritty floor. He groans loudly, clutching his chest, feeling his heart pound like an off-balance washer in spin cycle.

Not long after, his worries about Stan's jealousy and The Press's finances become, in effect, irrelevant.

THANKS TO THE Internet, within hours the news sweeps over the publishing community like a tsunami: a famous literary agent, a senior fiction editor, and a publisher have died from apparent poisoning. The literary agent's clients frantically dig out their contracts looking for a death clause (there isn't one). The editor's friends blog tearful eulogies recalling their common love of scrap booking and Chihuahuas. The publisher's death seals the suspicion that the entire industry is under siege from terrorists.

Then the rumor spreads: the three victims ingested arsenic from the *glue of a self-addressed stamped envelope.* Traces of the poisoned glue have been found on their tongues. Hundreds of fragile agent-author relationships dissolve from mistrust. Paranoid editors view each query like a live grenade. Interns refuse to lick, ever again. The more astute writers run out and buy self-sealing self-addressed stamped envelopes, or SSSASEs, to improve their chances in the slush pile.

NYPD DETECTIVE MIKE McIntyre is assigned to investigate the three homicides. He scans the lab report on the doctored envelopes, which have been returned, "address unknown," to their three (dead) senders. Their sticky edges were laden with arsenic trioxide.

Mike begins with the apartment of the famous literary agent. He pulls aside the yellow tape and surveys her living room. The first thing he notices is the mountain of unanswered mail. He imagines his own query letter is buried in there somewhere. He wrote a police procedural, a story of gangs, drugs, and corruption á la Joseph Wambaugh. He spent three years writing and revising, then another year fruitlessly looking for an agent before abandoning his dream of early retirement and a beach house in the Outer Banks. He knows he queried the famous literary agent but doesn't think she responded. He sniffs in disapproval, knowing each letter represents a person who'd reached out to the famous literary agent in vain, begging for a kind word of validation. The mountain of letters represent a pile of broken dreams and broken hearts. A pile of suspects? *Did a writer commit this murder?*

Mike sifts, reads, and speculates that highly offended writers would come in three flavors: ignored, rejected, and mistreated. He calls for assistance and a uniformed cop shows up; together they go through every scrap of paper in the pile, logging names and addresses.

Next, he sorts through her project files. Mike recognizes the name of her star client, Quincy Quaid, author of over a hundred romance novels, many of them best-sellers. Quaid's folders fill an entire file drawer, with contracts for foreign rights and movie options and even merchandise deals. Whew, lookee that: a promotions budget that exceeds his detective's salary. Nice. He shoves the folder back into the cabinet and goes out to pay a visit to the offices of The Press.

"EVERYONE'S BEEN MURDERED, how do you think I feel?" The Press's only remaining employee—an editorial assistant—wears excessive eyeliner and a silver stud in her slightly inflamed upper lip. A tattoo of a dolphin leaps out of her cleavage.

Mike feels repelled and confused. And old. "Can I get a list of Press authors?"

She leans onto one curvy haunch as she paints her nails a shiny black, probably not in mourning. "Going back how long?"

He shrugs. "Ten years?"

She waves her talons in the air to dry them, then turns to her computer and begins typing, the clicks of her fingernails hitting the keys like corn popping. "My question is, like, will I get a paycheck this week? Cause I have, like, bills. And I haven't been paid in a month." The printer spits out three pages, and she hands them to Mike.

"Who would want to cause . . ." (he almost says "like") " . . . harm to the Press?"

She pushes silky hair behind her curled-shell-like ears and taps the stud in her lip. It looks painful. "Omigod. It was high drama around here 24-7. New boyfriends, old boyfriends, bill collectors, banks cutting us off, writers wanting their money. Better than a soap opera. But murder? I don't *think* so."

Mike scans the list of Press authors. Three of them are also clients of the famous literary agent.

QUINCY QUAID'S APARTMENT smells like Raid and cat. The source of the latter odor, a yellow kitty with fur as fluffy as a dandelion, drapes itself at Mike's feet and begins a rumbly purring as he rubs its head. Quincy Quaid is a delicate petite woman with a writhing mass of blonde hair, too much make-up, and a fluttering manner. "You're a big strapping fellow, aren't you? My, yes, nothing wussy about you. You may call me Quincy." She gives his knee a flirtatious squeeze but he senses that her heart isn't in it; her face is ashen, her eyes bloodshot.

"It's almost as though your career was a target," he says.

A tear slides down her cheek, carrying a speck of mascara with it. "I can't go on. My creative spirit is broken."

He feels a stab of sympathy; she seems fragile and vulnerable. "That would be a shame. I've enjoyed your books."

"Mike, I'm terrified. I keep thinking they died because of me! Meanwhile, I'm not licking any envelopes!" She half-laughs, half-shudders.

HE TAKES THE subway to the address of the next author, a disheveled man reeking of bourbon, never a good sign at ten a.m. The writer shoos a tuxedo cat off the couch then clears a space by pushing aside an accumulation of unread newspapers, mail, beer cans, and pizza boxes. "Sit here. Want a drink?"

Mike declines. The writer picks up a glass of something that looks like water, but isn't, and takes a goodly swallow before he says, "I'll confess to an abiding, deep, permanent hatred for all three of them."

"*I* confess I haven't read your book."

"You and the rest of the English-speaking world. Does literary scandal sell books? The question wasn't answered, because The Press pulled back all copies and burned them."

"A memoir?"

"It was fiction, baby, utter fiction. I'm a great writer, and it was a great story. But I'm a bald dork from Ohio and nobody wanted it. So screw 'em, I rewrote it as memoir, sent it to the dead agent who sold it in an auction to the dead publisher, to be edited by the dead editor. All three well aware it was fiction."

Mike knows the book's premise: a married couple, parents of four kids, find out they are siblings. The writer had written it as the story of his parents, a tragic yet vaguely icky tale. "So it wasn't true? Your parents weren't brother and sister?"

"You're sharp, Sherlock. That's what I said. Fiction. And those three left me nailed to a cross to die for their sins."

"So you hated them."

"Makes me a suspect, right?" He holds out trembling hands as if to be cuffed.

"Did you kill them?"

"No. But I'll shake the hand of the sorry bastard who did it."

Mike isn't sure he is telling the truth. "I'll be in touch," he says. Should he come back with a search warrant? Somewhere in this sad clutter, would they find traces of arsenic trioxide?

HE PHONES THE third writer on both lists, a child psychologist from Charleston, the author of five books of advice for parents, starting with *Baby Your Baby* and ending with *Talk to Your Teen*. She has a breathy sexy voice with an accent marinated in grits, collards, and 'que. "Ah'm devastated. Ah'm readin' galleys and suddenly the rug's yanked and bam, Ah'm flat on ma ass with no agent and no publisher."

Envisioning a pissed-off Daisy Mae in horn-rims, Mike apologizes for the intrusion and asks if she knows of any conflicts involving the victims.

"Absolutely not. We were a team, Mike. Teamwork is what Ah'm preaching in ma new book, *Families That Flourish*. But now ma team is gone and ma book with it." She whispers, "Ah cain't talk about it now, darlin'. Ah have to take ma kitty to the vet." Mike hears a mournful piercing howl that gives him chills. What is it with writers and cats?

STAN, THE CLUB performer and new friend of the now-dead publisher, isn't surprised that the detective wants to talk with him. He has *mad* ideas for who might have murdered his sweetheart and is *dying* to share them with a professional.

The detective is a bit overweight but in a firm not flabby way, with a nice face, kind of chiseled and Roman. Stan's tortie cat likes him too; she weaves around his legs.

"The neighbors heard you arguing," the detective says.

Stan jumps to his feet in horrified astonishment. "We were arguing? Discussing our feelings! That's what people do who care about each other!" He can't believe he might be a suspect. "Furthermore, I never even met that editor. Why would I kill someone I didn't know?"

The detective shrugs his broad shoulders. "Accident, maybe. What were you two arguing about all night?"

Stan almost forgets his loss for a moment, so wrought up by the unfairness of it all. Also, he is sidetracked by the detective's pecs and quads. Yummy. Too bad the fellow is a *cop*; Stan could get arrested, he supposes, for the slightest insinuation of a proposition. This dating thing is damned tricky, like traveling a pot-holed rutted highway, a dangerous bumpy journey almost not worth the effort. So when he'd met the publisher (now dead) and they'd hit it off so well (except for the intrusive presence of the publisher's ex-wife, also now dead), he'd been so relieved, so glad to have someone who'd understand his emotional needs, assuage his fear of abandonment, tolerate his moodiness and outbursts. In return he had complimented the publisher's gowns and make-up, suggesting in the most gently tactful way styles that flattered, that disguised the publisher's burly body and stumpy legs. Now the detective is asking *him* about the deaths, as though he's Snow White's stepmom slipping poisoned apple slices into everyone's lunch box.

"I loved him," Stan says, "we were like that," waggling his crossed fingers. "You can't possibly believe I would do anything violent."

"Poisoning isn't violent, actually. It's indirect, removed," the dreamy cop says.

"Semantics. I could never murder anyone." He closes his eyes to shut out the distracting man in a well-cut suit—clothes are *so* important—and thinks about his friend the publisher, now dead, gone forever. He is alone, again. Tears well up in his eyes and he pinches his nose to stop them.

THE WRITER NOTICES new tremor in hands. Must taper Xanax. One more letter to prepare, difficult with shaking hands. The cat jumps on the counter, almost spills little jar of powder. Writer shrieks, "Get away!" and then feels bad for yelling at the cat. Lick & stick glue is a great invention. The writer feels stressed.

Doorbell rings and the writer opens door to the hot detective and a uniformed cop pointing a gun. Detective doesn't miss a trick. The writer is afraid that what is to come will be horrible. The writer runs into kitchen, picks up little jar of powder and throws a good bit down throat. Curious how arsenic trioxide is tasteless.

The detective calls for an ambulance, takes writer in his arms and asks why? The writer explains, enjoys the snuggle, for a little while.

THEY WATCH THE ambulance take the body away, and then the uniformed cop begins to cordon off the apartment with yellow tape. "It looked like she was preparing another envelope," he says.

"For her ex-husband," Mike says. "She told me she was empty, she had to get off the treadmill of four books a year. But she owed so much money she couldn't afford to get out of her contracts. Somehow, she thought that murdering her publishing team would end her problems."

The uniformed cop, who wants to be a homicide detective someday, has been following the case. "What made you suspect Quincy Quaid?"

"The lab found yellow cat hairs on one of the doctored envelopes. I obtained cat hairs from the most likely suspects, and only Quincy's cat was a match." Mike reaches down to pat the cat's thick golden fur.

"One of the writers lived in Charleston, didn't she? You didn't go there."

"I heard her cat yowl and that was enough—it was a Siamese."

Seriously impressed, the uniformed cop realizes there is more to detecting than wearing a well-cut suit.

Hidden

MEMORY IS A funny thing these days. I forget appointments, misplace keys, wander about Kroger's parking lot looking for my car. But the past springs to life vividly, sparked by the smallest nothing. Combing my short gray hair, I fall into a memory of Emma, her musical Dutch-accented voice muttering as she detangled and braided my hair. I hear the bark of a nervous dog and my heart races, remembering Rudi's sharp yip-yip of warning. When I walk with my grandchildren through the woods near their home, a sudden rustle from the underbrush bathes me in adrenaline, my breath quickens and I fight the urge to run. And smells! Sardines, starch, Pall Mall cigarettes—all carry me to long ago and far away.

IN MAY 1942, after our father died in a sea battle, Mama, Giles, and I left our home in Rouen and went to live with Grand-papa in a village outside Lille. His house was tiny, with only two rooms; mattresses on the floor in one room, a stove and table in the other.

It was an unhappy time. There were no servants, and Mama had too much work to do. She hated cooking and besides, food was scarce. She fixed brick-hard bread, applesauce, carrots, and eggs, always eggs. Grand-papa drank apple brandy all day and fussed at me for being loud and bouncy. But what was I to do? I missed my friend Anna, our games in the schoolyard, ballet lessons. I pouted and whined until Mama said, "Leni, your incessant crying is making me crazy. Go into the bedroom, shut the door, and count your blessings."

"What blessings?" I shouted between dramatic sobs. "The Nazis want to kill us!" I slammed the door and buried my wet face in sour-smelling blankets. "I hate it here! I hate my life!" My tears flowed until I was bored and went out to find Giles.

I would pester Giles, follow him into the woods, down to the trickle of a creek, watch him climb and dig holes and catch tiny fish. He was thirteen and I was seven, a mile-wide chasm. If Giles ever humbled himself to play with me, we constructed forts, stocked them with stick-guns and knives. I had to be the Nazi soldier. The soldier ran, hid, was caught and tied up with rope. Giles was cowardly in most situations, but brave enough to capture this little Nazi.

In the village, real Nazis stood on the sidewalk, looking us over, staring at the yellow stars on our coats with sour expressions on their cold faces. One of Giles's eyes wandered outward, especially when he was anxious or upset, and he was self-conscious, worried a soldier would notice him. He had a bad stutter, and the Nazis knew it. "B-b-b-bumble b-b-b-bee eyes," they jeered, as Giles lurked behind Mama and me. "Stand tall," Mama told him, but he skulked along, like he was trying to be invisible.

ONE DAY A man in a black suit drove up to Grand-papa's house.

"The doctor will take you to a place where you will be safe," Mama said.

Giles said, "I won't g-g-g-go. I'll run away. He'll take us to a c-c-c-camp to be k-k-k-killed!" His stutter was worse when he was upset.

We had heard stories of trains to death camps. It scared me that he was so upset. Mama calmed us, saying, "You will be safe. The Nazis won't find you. I promise."

We put on almost all our clothes until we looked like stuffed bears. I clutched my doll, Giles carried a small suitcase. His face was white and stony. Mama stood at the iron gate, blew kisses, smiled, though her face was wet with tears.

The doctor unpinned the yellow stars from our coats. He told us, "At the checkpoints, I will say I am taking you to a hospital. You must pretend to be sick. Cover up with blankets until you are hot and feverish-looking. Close your eyes and be very quiet."

Wearing so many clothes, I was burning up and it was easy to look hot. The doctor drove for hours, it seemed, until reaching a small farm on the outskirts of a Belgian village.

Be very quiet. A order we were to live by.

"CALL ME TANTE," the woman said, though she was not our aunt. She helped us remove most of our clothes, clucked and hissed, "Too thin!" After a meal of fried sausage and potatoes, she led us to her bedroom, opened a hatch in the ceiling, and pulled down a ladder. She shooed us into an attic, a dirty space filled with boxes, bundles, and broken furniture. There was a window with a black curtain, and a pile of blankets for a bed.

"You will stay here, because people gossip and there are collaborators," Tante said. "Never come down unless I tell you."

In the corner of the attic stood a tall oak dresser and next to it, a stovepipe through the floor and up out the roof. She stooped and reached behind the stovepipe, tugged on a board until a cupboard door opened, revealing a dark space under the sloped roof.

"Here's your hidey-hole," she said. "You can latch it securely once you are inside. No one will know you are here if you are quiet. Go on, try it out."

The hidey-hole had a low ceiling but was big enough for Giles and me to lie down, elbow to elbow. We both sneezed from the dust. I began to cry. I missed my mother, I was afraid, and I didn't want to live in a dirty attic. Giles tried to shush me, sang silly songs, but I wailed until Tante climbed the ladder and poked her head into the hidey-hole. "The Nazis will hear you," she said, "and we will all be shot. Be very quiet."

Many times Tante fussed at me for crying. I learned to cry in silence.

TANTE WORE THICK glasses, fixed her black hair in tidy braids wrapped round her head, and spoke with a strong Dutch accent. Her husband and three sons had been forced into factories in Germany. She worked the small farm with her father, Opa, and

Emma, her sixteen-year-old daughter. The farm was perhaps five acres, with a chicken coop, rabbit hutches, and bee boxes. There was a small barn, a pasture for two cows, and a large garden for growing potatoes, beans, cabbage, carrots, beets. Their nervous cloudy-eyed dog, Rudi, walked slow from arthritis, and barn cats showed up every evening for pans of milk but scattered at the approach of people.

Opa was old, white-haired and bent over. He walked with a stick, but never rested until evenings. Then he sat by the stove and listened to Radio Belgique, turned low because it was forbidden, growling curses at the Boches until Tante shushed him.

Emma had thick chestnut hair in a complicated braid woven around her head. She was jolly with rosy cheeks and, like Tante and Opa, never stopped in the daytime–cooking, baking, cleaning, washing. Tante and Emma spent mornings outside in the garden, weeding, picking fruits and vegetables, then pickling and canning them. In the cellar they buried cabbage and turnips, laid out potatoes, onions, and carrots in boxes. Opa tended the rabbits and bees, repaired tools, hunted wild hogs in the oak forest beyond the pasture.

Tante promised to fatten us up. Giles joked we were like Hansel and Gretel, prisoners of a witch who will cook and eat us. His stutter was worse, or perhaps I just noticed more, being shut up with him all day and night.

We became Emma's project. She climbed the ladder with a food bucket and climbed back down with the shit bucket. Giles said it was shameful work for her, emptying that bucket. She was kind and cheerful, never severe like Tante. When the terrible smell of his feet made me gag, Emma filled a bowl with hot water and vinegar and he soaked his feet. It worked! Giles said we made a lot of extra work for her.

The attic's one grimy window was stuck closed but we folded back the cloth covering a bit to peek out: at Tante in the garden, Emma walking the cows to the barn at dusk, a person riding past on a bicycle. Sometimes we saw children and I was so sad, missing Anna, missing our play with our dolls under the lilac bushes behind her house. We couldn't even write letters to our mother, Emma said, since not even the postman could know about us. But on each of our birthdays—three of them—somehow Mama managed to get us a letter and some sweets.

AFTER DARK, TANTE allowed us to come down the ladder and put us to work. My chore was churning butter, to burn up my energy; Giles helped Opa outside. Afterward we played tag and climbed the fruit trees. Giles wanted to explore the oak forest but Opa said, "No, the wild hogs will eat you."

Rudi was a good watch dog, with different barks for neighbors and strangers. The bark for neighbors was a deep woof woof. His tail wagged, and his ears perked up. He greeted strangers with a higher-pitched bark, a yip-yip, and he was stiff and alert. We knew to be quiet when someone approached; no one must know we hid in the attic.

As an extra signal, Tante banged a pot on the wood stove.

Two *clanks* meant *be very quiet.* Someone was coming, to talk, or to buy eggs or honey.

Clank-clank-clank meant *German soldiers, go into the hidey-hole.* Giles said, "They are d-d-d-devils and I wish I had a gun."

Five quick *clanks* meant *all clear.*

I WAS ALWAYS frightened. I didn't sleep soundly; even dreaming, I was alert to small noises. The loud hoots of owls would wake me. One perched right outside our window and others answered it from the woods. During the night, Rudi barked, at stoats, deer, squirrels. In the dark attic, with only a crack in the curtain to allow moonlight, things in the room seemed to move. The floor moved like quicksand, a witch hid behind a chair, a bundle was full of slugs and snakes. Hands with long fingers worked the attic hatch. Nightmares took me down into dark places until I woke, terrified, grunting strangled screams. (Even asleep I remembered to keep quiet.)

Then I would sit by the window to watch the stars slowly rotate in the sky, clouds pass before the face of the moon. I wondered if

Mama saw them too; maybe we watched together. Often, a pack
of wild hogs came to dig for acorns beneath the giant oak in front
of the house. Then, like Giles and me, Rudi was very quiet, holed
up in his dog-house next to the chicken pen.

LATE ONE MORNING Emma brought us a can of sardines,
drizzled with vinegar. At the sight of the little black-eyed silver
fish, I cried and refused to eat them but Giles said they tasted
so good, mashed on a piece of toast, and after one little bite I
decided yes, they were delicious. We were licking our fingers
when came *clank-clank-clank*. My heart beat with a terrible
fright and I began to cry, I couldn't stop. Tante made Emma
go in the hidey-hole with us, to calm me. Two soldiers stomped
about below, talking harshly to Tante. Giles and I understood
a little German—our grandfather had spoken German to our
mother. The soldiers said Tante must give them butter, rabbit
meat, and eggs every week. She will have to meet a quota.

The hidey-hole was hot as an oven. We lay quiet until the
stomping and the voices ceased. *Clank* five times. I sat up,
dripping with sweat. My heart would not slow down.

The soldiers took—no, *stole*—eggs, honey, jars of pickles and
beans, and three loaves of bread that had been cooling.

PASSING THE TIME was so difficult. I made paper dolls,
drew pictures. We played checkers. Emma brought us arithmetic
and history books. Giles taught me a bit of English and read
Alice's Adventures in Wonderland aloud to me. We studied a book
of maps over and over, planning where we'd go. *After*. We listed
ways to kill Nazis. Sharp things to stab them with: knives of
course, ice picks, spears, arrows. Hard things like hammers to
bash their brains out. Ropes, scarves, wire, string to strangle
them with.

We talked constantly of *after*. After this, after the war, after
the Nazis all died. It helped, to think about a future.

EVERY WEEK, THE German soldiers, always the same two, came on motorbikes for Tante's food. Spots was tall and pimply, Tiny Eyes had slicked-back black hair and, well, tiny eyes set back in his skull. After the first few times, as soon as Rudi began to yip and we heard the putt-putt of their bikes, Tante made Emma go into the hidey-hole with us.

Emma would lie squished between Giles and me, her eyes closed, her cheeks pale. She smelled like sweat and starch. I lay rigid, too frightened to sleep, breathing a sort-of prayer, angels surround us. *Anges nous entourent.* I imagined enchanted glowing creatures, their silver swords poised to protect. I buried my face against Emma's arm, silently wetting her sleeve with my tears.

Giles too turned his face toward Emma, watching her with one eye as the other wandered upward to the spider-webbed ceiling.

I thought she was there to shush us.

WE WERE NOT the only hidden ones. Through cracks in the floorboards, we heard hushed talk about Allied airmen moving from farm to farm, eventually to Paris and escape routes into Spain. We were intensely curious but also afraid, because Tante, Opa, and Emma would tell us nothing, and their silence only added to my worry.

Moving some boxes and bundles around in the attic, I found a wood rocking chair with arms and a carved back. One runner was missing, and Opa fixed it for me. I rocked all day, cradling my doll. Creak creak creak creak . . . Giles didn't protest.

OUR THIRD WINTER was frigid with lots of snow. Snow covered the farm, the road, and the barn with a pure white thick blanket. Another time, it would seem magical to us. But two feet of snow was no protection against Nazis, or a witch behind the chair, a floor of quicksand. The owl was just as loud, the dog just as nervous.

On the evening before his sixteenth birthday, Giles was shoveling paths through the yard, to the road, the barn, the rabbit, and chicken coops, when Rudi began to bark. Giles ran into the house. A neighbor from a nearby farm had made his way through drifts and Opa let him in. We tried to overhear what they talked about, but they went outside, to the barn, without speaking.

I went back to my sketches. I was drawing a bouquet of flowers for Giles, for his birthday. Tante promised an apple tart, and Emma was making over some clothes of her father's for him.

That night, Tante made us stay in the attic instead of coming down for chores, play, and warm milk. She didn't explain, but said firmly, "Be very quiet."

It was late, after curfew, when Rudi started to bark again. *Strangers.* "Something's going on," Giles said, and we crowded together to peek out the window. A half-moon cast a dim light over the yard, crisscrossed with shoveled paths. Two men walked into the yard. Opa went outside, hushed the dog, and led the men into the barn.

"Nazis?" I asked. "Should we get into the hidey-hole?"

"No. Civilians," Giles said. "Wait and see." His voice was a man's, now.

One man came out of the barn and walked away. Opa returned to the house. We put our ears to the floor to listen, and heard Emma ask, "Who is he?"

Opa said, "An American airman. He has a concussion."

"Oooo," Tante said. I could almost see her pursed lips and frowning eyes.

Giles and I looked at each other with big eyes. An airman! An American!

"He will stay here at least a few days," Opa said. "Then he'll be taken to Paris."

"The Germans will be looking for him," Emma said.

"Of course," Opa said. "But Adrian burned his parachute and clothing, and we have hidden him well."

"He will want to eat," Tante said. We heard the crackle of potatoes dropped into hot oil. Tante made the best fries.

"I want to see him," Giles whispered to me.

I nodded. An American airman!

THE NEXT DAY we were crazy to see the airman but Emma said, "It is too dangerous, for him and for you. What if he was captured? He might tell about you two." She had helped me bathe, and was trying to comb my hair, not an easy job. It was so long, almost to my waist, and tangled easily. But she was patient, working on it strand by strand.

"He wouldn't tell," Giles said. "He is a b-b-b-brave man."

She looked up at him, shook her head, then went back to combing.

"Don't tell him we're Jewish," I said. "Tell him we are your sister and brother."

"P-p-p-please?" Giles begged.

"No. It's not safe for you or him."

I was wildly disappointed, sick of being *safe*.

SO, THE NEXT afternoon, when Tante and Opa had gone somewhere on the train, and Emma was in the garden, Giles and I crept out of the house and dashed into the barn. Cats scattered as we tiptoed around looking for the airman, going from stall to stall, climbing to the loft, peeking into cupboards. We couldn't find him! Emma caught us coming out of the barn.

"Idiots," she said. "What are you doing?" She carried a pan of rabbit meat.

Giles shrugged. "Nothing. Just looking in the b-b-b-barn."

Emma looked us up and down. Giles had grown a good six inches taller, and his pants barely covered his knees. "What did you find?" she asked.

"Cats," I said. "Many cats."

"Good. Now back inside. I'll bring you some stew later."

Just then, Rudi's sharp yip-yip and the rumble of a motorbike coming down the road jolted us into a panic, and we ran across the yard, inside, and up into the attic. Giles pulled up the ladder, and we squatted by the window and opened the curtain a tiny sliver to see who it was. Tiny Eyes, by himself. He banged on the door and Emma let him in. We crept into our hidey-hole. My heart thumped the way it always did when a Nazi soldier was in the house.

"Is he looking for the airman?" I whispered.

"He asks her for the food," Giles told me. He frowned. I could hear arguing and Emma yelling, "No, stop."

"What shall we do?" I whispered. "What's he doing?"

We heard thuds, like chairs falling over, and Emma screeched, "No, no!" The soldier yelled, "Quiet, you bitch!" and more thuds then suddenly she was silent.

"Has he left?" I whispered.

Giles was so red I thought he would ignite. He opened the door to the hidey-hole. "Stay here," he said.

But I followed, scrambling down the ladder. Whatever was happening, I wanted to be part of it.

The soldier was on top of Emma, on the floor, struggling with her. He had one hand around her throat, and the other pulling on her clothes, and she squealed and squirmed, pushing against him. His pants were down and his bare bottom shoved against her. It was a horrible sight and as I started to cry, Giles lifted Tante's big black fry pan and swung it onto the side of the soldier's head, knocking his face into the floor. Giles whammed the fry pan into the soldier's head over and over as Emma wriggled away and her noises changed from squeals to sobs, just one or two, then she stopped. Emma was as tough as they come.

The soldier lay still. Blood poured from his head. "He's dead," Emma said, but when Giles nudged him with his foot, the soldier moaned. He wasn't dead. More blood. Oh, so much blood. The soldier's pants were clumped around his ankles, and I couldn't help seeing his stiff penis, like a mule's, in its hairy nest. Disgusting. Poor Emma.

She was all right. "You two saved me," she said. "He didn't get very far." She took our hands—Giles's all bloody and sticky and trembling—and we stood, joined in a circle, over the soldier's body, until she kicked him, then I gasped and kicked him too. Oh, how Emma and I kicked that Nazi soldier until our shoes were bloody. We tried to be quiet, choked on strangled laughter, excited, though I wanted to shriek to the heavens *Filthy Boche! Dead Nazi!* Giles backed away, watching us celebrate. When the Nazi stopped moaning, Emma and I turned to Giles to praise his bravery, but he stood rigid and the color was gone from his face.

"They will hang us from trees for this," he said. "Your mama and *grand-père* too. They will find the airman and shoot him."

"No. He will help us," Emma said, and she darted outside.

We listened to the soldier gurgle through his broken nose. "You were brave," I said to Giles. He ignored me and walked back and forth.

Emma came back with the airman. He was sandy-haired and stocky, and there was a big lump on his forehead. At the sight of the Nazi, he took out a cigarette and lit it.

"Nice job," he said. "Who are you?" His French was very good.

"I am Giles, and this is my sister Leni," Giles said.

"That's a Nazi soldier," I said. "He was hurting Emma and Giles hit him!"

"Good for Giles," the airman said. "Let's get rid of the bastard."

"Get rid of the bastard," I yelled. Emma grinned. She went into her bedroom, came out with a sheet. The airman and Giles rolled the Nazi onto the sheet, wrapped him up. He was still breathing. They dragged the bundled soldier outside, and I watched through the open back door as they heaved him through the yard, past the chicken pen, the garden, the bee houses, the sheds and into the woods.

Emma fetched cloths and a bucket of water. "We have to clean this up," she said. "They'll be looking for him." I set to work, frantically sopping up bloody water, emptying the bucket, filling it again, over and over. We washed the floor, cupboards, our shoes, the wood stove, chair legs until every speck of blood was gone. She wrung out the cloths, put them into soapy water along with the small rag rug that lay before the sink.

We sat by the attic window, hip to hip, and waited. I lay down onto Emma's lap, but my muscles felt tight and shivery and I couldn't rest.

It was dark when Giles and the airman came back. They stopped in the yard and pumped water to wash, and I climbed down the ladder and ran out to them, crying, so glad the Nazis hadn't caught them and hung them from a tree.

"Where's your mom? The old guy?" The airman asked. He squatted to rub Rudi's ears.

"They will be back late tonight," Emma said. "Come in, have something to eat." She cut bread, spread butter and jam.

"What did you do with the Nazi?" I asked.

Giles and the airman shared a glance. Giles said, "We took him very far into the trees, burned his clothes, then waited."

"For what?"

"For the hogs to smell his blood."

The airman shook his head and said, "We got pigs back home, but I never saw them do a man like that."

A feeling of glee stabbed me. Glee on top of terror and exhaustion, and I couldn't help it, I let go of a warm gush of pee, pee I'd been unable to release all day.

"Poor girl," Emma said. "But that will explain the wet rags, and the clean floor. Now go up to bed."

THE AIRMAN LEFT with the motorbike.

"Where's he going?" I asked.

"To ditch it," Giles said. "So no one will know Tiny Eyes was here."

"Is he coming back?"

"I don't know."

I pulled a blanket around me and curled onto the rocking chair. I was wide awake, worried about the airman. When Rudi woofed softly, I peeked out the window; the moon was bright enough to see Tante and Opa, returning in the mule-driven wagon. Emma had said it was better that they didn't know what happened, and we should say nothing to them.

Then I must have slept because the next thing I knew, the hatch to the attic was opening and the airman was climbing through it. "Hey there, kids," he said. "There's German soldiers coming up the road and the old man told me to hide up here with you two."

"You had a good hiding place in the barn," Giles said. "We couldn't find you."

"I wasn't in the barn. I was off in the woods having a smoke because the old man told me not to smoke in the barn. Anyway, what's the plan up here?"

"Follow me," I said, and opened the cupboard to our hidey-hole. We crawled in, latched the door, and lay down with the airman in the middle, squashed together in a sandwich. My head was under his arm, and I could feel his heart thump, his ribs move as he breathed. He smelled of cigarettes, of hay, and leaves.

Rudi barked hysterically as motorbikes pulled into the yard. *Bam-bam* pounding on the door, then sharp voices questioning Tante about Tiny Eyes. She would be in her nightdress and robe, black braids hanging down.

"No, no soldiers were here today," she told them. "Should I wake my old father and child?"

The soldiers stomped through the kitchen, into the small parlor, then outside. As Rudi barked and barked, I guessed they were searching the barn. We lay in silence until we heard the motorbikes putt-putt away.

"We'll live another day, guys," the airman said. "Say, how long you been hiding here?"

"Almost three years," I said.

"The war's almost over," he said. "We're bombing the shit out of Berlin."

My brave brother Giles smiled, and I felt my muscles uncoil, for the first time since I put on all my clothes for the car ride from Lille. I stretched a little to get more comfortable, and rested my head on the airman's chest. His heart had slowed, but I could still feel it thumping beneath the scratchy wool of his shirt. *Anges nous entourent,* I breathed, closing my eyes to conjure up flickering lights, tiny silver swords.

The airman asked what I had said.
"*Anges nous entourent,*" said Giles.
"Indeed they do," the airman said.

Have You Seen Her?

I REMEMBER EVERY detail of that last morning. I'd fixed pancakes and bacon for the three of us. Our seven-year-old, Connor, rocked in his squeaky chair, humming, lost in his crazy-boy thoughts. When sunlight struck a crystal hanging in the window, scattering rainbow flickers around the kitchen, he reached out his hands to catch the flying jewels. He hooted his excited-monkey noise until I silenced him with the last piece of bacon.

After a twelve-hour patrol shift, Greg looked drained, even with the rainbow glimmering across his face. Budget cuts had reduced the police force, but not the workload. Just as many folks gone adrift as ever.

"I'll take him to the beach park this morning. You get some rest," I said.

Greg kissed my ear. "You're a keeper," he said, his breath sour and warm. He started loading the dishwasher but I shooed him out of the kitchen.

AT THE PARK Connor would swing happily as long as I kept pushing him, and though after the thousandth shove on his bony bottom I was exquisitely bored, it was a good day to be alive, to enjoy the ocean's sparkle, the cries of gulls, the fresh iodine-smell of the sea.

We were alone until a girl sat on the swing next to Connor. Pleased at the diversion, I was a bit puzzled at her appearance out of nowhere; I hadn't noticed her approach though the area around the swings was open space. Her golden hair was long, dirty, and tangled. She wore a grimy white dress and black leggings with lace trim, and was barefoot. If cornered in a witness box I would put her age at ten, though she was slight and could be any age, even twenty. Alone, thin and dirty—at first, I felt a pang of sympathy.

Though she hadn't made a sound, Connor twisted toward her, dragging his feet to slow his swing. He smiled. Was he smiling *at* her?

Then a miracle occurred. "Hi," said my nonverbal son. "I'm Connor."

You can't imagine what joyful emotion flooded me at this instant as I realized that he'd spoken *to* someone. This girl had triggered something in him that a dozen therapists had tried and failed. He was being *social*.

She turned to us. Her features are hazy in my memory but there was something compelling about her and I stared at her until I realized what it was. Her eyes were solid black, reflective like marbles. Her eyes were all I noticed about her face.

When my gaze dropped to her dirty bare feet, my vision blurred. Were those claws? I blinked. No. Scaly, pointed toes. I felt pity, curiosity, and revulsion, and hoped my feelings didn't show. Though I was happy—and proud!—that my son had made a connection with another person, I had trouble believing what I saw—the strangeness of the girl's eyes and Connor's recognition of her were too far from my everyday normal.

"Can I go home with you?" she asked. "I'm hungry." Her voice was low, confident, and too mature for a child. As though she knew her eyes alarmed me, she half-closed them and looked away. A feeling of dread fell over me, my instincts whispered *she is something other* and I made a decision.

"No. Leave us alone." I turned my back to her, tugged Connor from his swing, and trotted to my car. Usually he was limply docile, but he could be a handful when he was balked, and he struggled, kicked me and wailed. Adrenaline made me shaky and I fumbled as I buckled him into his seat.

The girl stood close behind me. "Please? Take me with you." Her thin body drooped, her voice a hoarse whisper.

"Get away." I slid into my car and locked the doors. She leaned toward my window, and her dirty gold hair fell about her pale face, framed her solid black eyes. As I drove away, I looked in the rearview mirror, then scanned the parking lot and beach. Like that old cliché, she'd vanished into thin air.

Connor's wailing intensified. He had an eerie cry, a high-pitched "eeeee" so painful you'd do anything to make it stop. He cried all the way home, where I had to hold him tight and rock him for almost an hour before he quieted down.

When I told Greg about the girl, he was skeptical and made jokes about broomsticks, aliens, and spaceships. I brooded, wished Greg had been with me to see what I saw. I locked all the doors.

IN THE AFTERNOON we took Connor to an appointment with his occupational therapist, where we watched him roll around in a ball pit, then refuse to button his shirt.

When we returned home, guess who was sitting on the porch?

"Oh, dear God. That's the girl from the park," I said. "Don't stop. Just drive off."

"Naw, she's a kid." He pulled into the driveway, and I shrank into my seat.

She came to Greg's side of the car. "I would like something to eat, please," she said, in her strangely adult voice. She studied Connor, who was asleep, with her coal-lump eyes. "Just a little something. I like cereal." She was so close I could see the dirt rings on her neck, her bumpy skin.

I grabbed Greg's arm. "Her eyes, Greg. Put your window up and lock your door."

Greg looked at me impatiently. "We can't sit here all day. And what's a little bit of cereal?"

He got out of the car and motioned her up the steps. When she followed him into our house, I slouched down and waited for my heart to slow its thumping. As minutes passed, I wondered whether I should check on them, but I didn't want to leave Connor sleeping in the car. To be honest, I didn't want to leave the car, period. The girl scared me. Greg feared very little; he was a big man, a cop, and didn't seem to sense what I did. And he took care of people, that was his nature.

By the time Connor woke up, writhing to be let out of his car seat, I decided that maybe I was a neurotic mess, afraid of someone who looked a little different, a dusty homeless girl with an unusual eye disease. Maybe this was the breakdown the therapists had warned me about: a caretaker's collapse, the result of ignoring myself for too many years. Feeling numb, I unbuckled Connor and took him inside.

The house was silent and cold. In the kitchen, a cereal bowl held a few soggy corn flakes and a trace of milk. I looked all over the house but they were gone. I tried to be calm, rational. Maybe she needed Greg's help, or had something important to show him. Surely he would return soon.

Connor rocked and hummed, his chair squeaked. I paced, sat, turned the TV on and off. I had a bad feeling and it got worse as the hours passed. I fixed a simple meal of chicken nuggets and green beans, but I couldn't eat, my stomach was like cement. Something had happened to Greg, but what? If I called for help, what would I say?

Darkness fell. When I pulled back Connor's blanket to tuck him into bed, on his pillow was a scarlet splotch the size of my hand that looked like blood. And a coarse gold hair.

I phoned the police. They came quickly; Greg was one of theirs.

IT WAS HARD to keep an eye on Connor; the cruiser's flashing lights lured him outside and he twirled around in the darkness while they questioned me. I was well aware the police didn't share my belief that the black-eyed girl was an evil being, an *other*. I knew how it sounded—my husband had gone off with a girl half my age. I was describing her for about the twentieth time when I sensed a blur of motion along the beach path, a glimpse of white dress, and saw my son run, flying to meet her, disappearing into the black vacuum of a moonless night.

Screaming Connor's name over and over, I ran after him, but in the pitch dark I tripped over a clump of roots and fell hard onto the sand, knocked breathless. Someone lifted me up. "My son," I gasped, pointed, "out there." They ran toward the beach.

I AM ALONE now. I hate this house because *she* was in it, but I can't move away because what if they come back?

Every day is the same. I fill a baggie with corn flakes, tug on my floppy blue hat and walk the narrow path that leads alongside my house, down to the beach where fishermen chat over bait buckets and the first beer of the day. Wave at the bowlegged, leathery jogger running barefoot along the tide line. Stoop down to pet the bulldog inspecting the spiked shell of a horseshoe crab.

The crystal hangs from my neck, sending rainbow flickers onto the sand, into the wind.

I walk. I walk for miles, past surfers, sunbathers, and couples, under boardwalks, around sand castles and tidal pools. I've become a fixture on the beach, the woman in the blue hat who walks all day and into the evening, and sometimes people join me. I tell them my husband and son are missing, and show them pictures of Greg and Connor.

I ask if they've seen the black-eyed girl. My memory has a blank hole, her features elude me and I can't tell you what she looked like, other than her solid black eyes, dirty gold hair, and pointed, scaly toes.

But that should be enough.

Snow Day

TOM AND I huddle close together in the bus stop shelter. Damp icy air, murky gray clouds. I hold out my hand to catch my first-ever snowflake. A real blizzard will churn across the state tonight. We expect a foot of snow and a deep freeze. Missouri winters are brutal. Coming from Florida where I never even wore a jacket, I have no doubt I'm about to experience a frosty death. I shiver, wish I had a winter coat, but after filling the propane tank and car repairs my parents are tapped out.

"Lulu, put this on." Tom tucks his heavy wool jacket over my shoulders.

It's warm from his body and I cover my face with it, inhale. "What about you?" I ask. My lovely boyfriend shrugs, hands in pockets. His tee-shirt won't keep out the cold. The snow picks up and begins to come down serious. I wrap my arms around him to keep half of him warm.

"Wish I could buy you a coat," he says. Tom is the best, but more broke you can't imagine. No jobs for teens in this town. His parents are splitting, it's high drama, wah-wah-wah all day about money. We're poor. It sucks.

The snow falls thickly, frosting his hair. He grabs my hand. "Let's get something to eat." He can eat every half-hour and my stomach's empty too.

I dig into my pocket. Eleven pennies and a dime, plus four quarters for laundry. "Uh, a donut?" Downtown shops are fancy, don't tolerate broke high school kids coming in to get out of the weather.

He laughs and shows me two dollar bills. "Tiffenee's Grill. It's warm and cheap. We'll share pancakes."

He pulls me around the corner and down a side street. Snowflakes float soft onto my face. We're jogging to keep warm when he stops at a lime-green door. Jet Rag, the store's called. In smudged windows, worn-out mannequins are wearing pilly Christmas sweaters, hideous with reindeer antlers, Santas and jingle bells. Did I say hideous? "My mom shops here," Tom says. "Maybe . . ."

The place smells funky. Old, sour, unwashed. It's even colder than outside—I can see Tom's breath. I don't care because the first thing I see is—omigod—a hand-lettered sign: "COATS 4 SALE $3" and I dive into the rack, searching for anything in size two. Or at least in that ballpark. I try on a down coat, puffy and red. Makes me look like a pillow with feet. An embroidered denim jacket—cool but hardly blizzard-proof. A stained trench coat hangs to my ankles.

"What about this one, Lu?" Tom holds up a gray wool coat, double-breasted, with nipped-in waist and flared skirt. Four fat black buttons. I put it on and gasp. It's vintage, warm, perfect. He kisses my forehead. "You look like Audrey Hepburn."

We hand over all our worldly cash. Even the pennies but it doesn't matter. I'm aglow with the thrill of the buy, the way I look and feel in the soft heathery tweed. From pitifully freezing to posh and warm, for three bucks.

I hand him his jacket, he slips it on. Outside, falling snow makes a whispery sound, turning the world a shushed white. I twirl, humming. Happy.

"Where to now, my elfin waif?" he asks.

My stomach rumbles. "A hot meal."

He raises an eyebrow. I laugh and show him the piece of paper I found in the pocket of my beautiful new coat. A picture of Andrew Jackson on one side, the White House on the other. "Take me to Tiffenee's, darling. For breakfast."

Side Effects

MY MOM POINTED to the wads of bandages on my wrists. "We were just getting used to the gay thing, and now this."

"Young lady, what's up?" The doctor leaned toward me. I held my breath to avoid inhaling his after-shave and looked away from the tufts of black hair sprouting from his ears.

"She's always been gloomy," my mom said. "She sees the worst."

I glared at her. I hated it when she talked about me like I wasn't in the room. "Life sucks," I muttered.

The doctor nodded. "Life does suck, sometimes."

"And then you die."

"Whoa. What about joy and pleasure?"

"Raindrops on roses? Humans abuse their gifts. Don't get me started on how they treat animals." I rubbed my arms where the adhesive itched.

"That is not your problem to solve. You are responsible for yourself only. And not doing so great a job of that."

North Carolina's Amendment One, denying the right of people like me to marry, pushed me to the edge. There I teetered until Mary Bee dumped me, fed up with my gloominess, dire predictions, and lack of humor. She'd told me to get help and when I argued with her she slammed her door in my face.

At the memory I wept, choking on the tears running down the back of my throat.

Dr. Klein said I needed electroconvulsive shock treatments to fry away my memories.

"You're treating my symptoms," I snuffled. "Not my disease."

"Dear child, your symptoms are your disease."

I couldn't argue. He was fifty-eight and his wall was papered with credentials. I was seventeen and failing high school. "I'll be a vegetable."

"No, no. You'll be a happy girl."

"Cabbages feel nothing."

My mom opened her pink trifold organizer and they selected a date.

A SMILING WOMAN with short brown hair sat on the foot of my bed. She wasn't a nurse or a doctor. She offered me a brownie. I knew what brownies were, but I didn't know who she was. My mind was working poorly—as though files were missing. My thoughts buzzed, searching for this person. She pulled out a pink trifold organizer, showed me the date, and said I'd been hospitalized for two weeks. Her hands looked familiar and it came to me then, that she was my mom.

"When can I go home?"

"When Dr. Klein says you're ready. He'll be along in a minute, we can ask him."

I closed my eyes. I was cured. I was fine. I practiced smiling and raising my eyebrows a bit. I wanted to look happy but not manic. Sunlight poured through my (barred and heavily screened) window and I got out of bed and pulled a chair into its warmth. But what was I wearing? Ruffle-trimmed pajamas with a teapot print?

"Mom, what the hell?"

"Sweetheart, they are lovely and comfortable."

"Sweats are comfortable. These are creepy."

She crossed her hands over her heart. "Thank God, you're better. Last week you didn't care what you wore."

A knock on the door, and the doctor poked his head in. His hairy knuckle beckoned my mom into the hall. My hearing was acute, and he wasn't even whispering. So I heard him say I needed another series, three more treatments, another week.

"She'll be so unhappy to hear that," my mom said.

"My point exactly," said Dr. Klein. "She's still unhappy. There's an alternative, no guarantees. A drug trial. It's up to you."

My mom looked at me and I nodded like a bobble doll. The doctor handed me a bottle of little green pills from a pharmaceutical company called Psylex. Take one a day with food. I accepted a brownie and popped a pill.

AT HOME, LYING on my bed, I studied my posters. Apparently my causes were the environment (a coral reef), gay rights (Matthew Shepard march), and revolutionaries (Mandela). Coral was dying, Matthew and Mandela dead. My newly electrolyzed and medicated self needed fresh issues, an update. Something more activist, more media-savvy.

A dog wandered in, a black lab with a whitish muzzle. Tail a-wagging, she laid her head on my knee. I stared at her for a while, finally remembering her name, Sydney. I searched my mind carefully, like you'd probe a tooth after a trip to the dentist. The pain was gone. My mind was filed off, filled in and smooth. I decided to take Sydney for a walk.

It may have been a mistake. All the houses were identical, all the streets looked alike. We walked and walked, Sydney padding along with her tongue hanging out. I asked a kid to bring the dog some water. I was just about to ask him to call my mom when I saw my brother Aaron washing his car. My twin, the successful one, six feet of prickitude.

"Can I borrow your car?" I asked. I wanted to drive by Mary Bee's house to see how it felt.

He barely looked up. "No, you're on medication."

Probably not the right medication, because I had an overwhelming desire to stab him with something pointy. Instead, friendly-like, I put a hand on his arm. "It's important. I really need to borrow your car." The air lit up with a golden glow and a melodic warbling. Dizzy, I put my other hand on his arm to steady myself, and the glow and singing intensified. It filled me with a rush of happiness.

He handed me the keys with a big smile. "Here you go! I'm going to Florida for spring break, so just keep it till I get back."

Reeling from the unexpected sensations and Aaron's bequest, I encountered my dad in the garage. Normally I avoided my dad, since it was painful to watch him pretend I wasn't a loser. "Hi, Dad," I mumbled, and he gave me a hug. The garage filled with twinkling light, accompanied by ethereal trilling.

I may have been forgetful and depressed, but I wasn't stupid. On a hunch, I asked him for money, expecting five bucks, but he emptied his wallet into my hand. "Need more than that?" He'd given me eighty dollars.

"Uh, yeah," I said, curious to see what would happen. He went into the house whistling and came back with a credit card. "Use this, honey. Have a good day."

EVERY DAY THAT I took a little green pill, my touch cut through people's bullshit resistance. They paid attention to me and followed my brilliant suggestions.

At first I worked it locally. My mother made me my favorite cake, coconut-lime. For extra credit to bring up my grade, my history teacher let me write about the Stonewall riots. I started a gay-straight alliance group and half the high school wanted to join for the dances and movie nights. A fist bump, a pat on the back, a handshake—and you were on my team.

I avoided Mary Bee though I missed her terribly. The only time I saw her was in American History class, first period. She sat two rows up, three seats over, a thousand miles away. Her hair was always slightly damp from her morning shower but I forgot how it smelled. Would she ever take me back? I wasn't gloomy any longer but a rejection could send me reeling into Dr. Klein's electron-rich clutches.

To take my mind off Mary Bee I decided to tackle some big problems. That was the way I rolled. My mom said that fretting obsessively about the impossible caused my depression. But Dr. K. said the depression was electro-chemical and I agreed. And now that I was better, I wanted to do good with my awesome new mojo. I knew I couldn't fix the world. But I could transform the minds of powerful people.

Spring break. Sydney and I took off in Aaron's car, fueled with my dad's Visa. I'd adjust some attitudes, starting with Buddy Palleson, the biggest real estate developer in New York City.

Palleson had an office in Miracle Towers on Fifth Avenue. I headed into the Towers Grill, pleased to learn they need help. The manager, a haggard smoker named Curtis, liked me. His eyes roamed all over me and he laughed at his own jokes until he choked for air. He gave me a job bussing tables and told me I could sleep on his couch for a couple of nights until I found a place. I'd been clearing tables for about an hour when Curtis backed me against the dishwasher and clutched my ass. "The boss is here and I'll introduce you if you're a good girl." His breath was lethal. I grabbed his wrists and pushed him off me, accompanied by soaring voices, sparkly lights. He led me to Palleson's private dining room and I shed my apron along the way.

As soon as we shook hands, Palleson was mine. He pulled out a chair. "Have a seat. Curtis, bring us some champagne. "

"I can't drink, I'm seventeen," I said. "How's about some OJ?"

"Put a drop of fizzy in it. Now what can I do for you?"

I laid it on pretty thick. His achievements, his reputation, his success. Blah, blah, blah. He wasn't bored with this. "What's left for you, Mr. Palleson? You're at a point in your life when you're questioning your purpose. It's time to give, so that your tombstone doesn't just say Rich Guy. You want it to say Saint." I took both his hands in mine, and the choir burst into song. I could hardly hear myself think.

He floated in the light, aglow, beaming joyfully at me. "Money's easy. It's the saint part that's hard."

"I have total faith in you, sir." I threw out some ideas for achieving sainthood. "What do poor kids need? A neighborhood library. Smaller classes. You could lobby for revised drug laws."

He shook his head. "Good ideas, dearie, but not up my alley. I'm in real estate."

I was silent, because I knew he'd get there.

"The words 'New York real estate' and 'help the needy' don't belong in the same sentence." He poked a finger at me for emphasis.

"The poor live somewhere, don't they?"

"The city puts them in hotels." He nodded at Curtis who trotted over. "Bring a dessert menu. She's a growing girl." He jabbed his finger at me again. "There's a bunch of abandoned apartments in the South Bronx and East Harlem. I look at them and smell failure. Rats. Broken elevators and falling down ceilings."

Time to seal the deal. I reached out and took hold of his hairy white arm just above his gold chain bracelet. A soprano sighed delicately, and silver specks floated through the air. "You should remodel them. It's your philanthropic duty as a New York real estate developer."

He jumped up. "You're right, by God. It's what I was put on earth for!"

Curtis brought me apple pie with vanilla ice cream and I ate it, content, listening to Buddy on the phone, to his bank, to the mayor, to his broker. He even called his senator and asked if there were Federal grants or tax credits for what he planned to do. He dictated a press release to his PR firm.

I thanked him for the pie.

"No, it's you I should be thanking. Who are you? I didn't even catch your name."

Curtis gave me a to-go cup of water for Sydney.

MY NEXT TARGET lived in Connecticut. Leigh Brackett was a self-promoting rightwingnut. The media loved her long blonde hair, cigar-smoking ways, and quotable rants. She was addicted to power but needed my help to jump to a new platform.

I lay down with Sydney in a juniper hedge behind a daffodil border. It was seven a.m., the hour that Leigh Brackett walked her dogs. When her two waddling corgis noticed Sydney, they dragged Leigh to the junipers. I stood up and said hello but she ignored me in a way that felt familiar. I noticed that she wasn't so horse-faced in person and she looked older than my mom. I needed to touch her but she kept backing away so I held out a felt-tip pen and the menu from the Miracle Towers Grill. "Miss Brackett, can I have your autograph? I'm such a fan."

She eyed the menu suspiciously. "What's that?"

"See, Buddy Palleson signed it too."

As she took the pen, my fingers brushed her hand. A ghostly soprano warmed up with minor arpeggios. The corgis stopped sniffing Sydney's butt and looked up at me through the glittering air for instructions.

"Sit," I told them. To Leigh, I said, "Your father loves you, you know."

Her face crumpled. "He—he—he's never said it!"

"Forgive him. He's a product of our misogynistic culture."

"How's that?" She took the tissue I offered and wiped her eyes.

"The Madonna-whore dichotomy. Where does a daughter fit in? He had no choice but to ignore you."

"He likes my books!"

"My point. You're trying to please him. What about Leigh?"

"I'm happy! Goddam happy!"

I let it lie there as she sobbed from the depths. Finally she caught her breath. "Everyone hates me except the weird ones who glom on."

"How's that working for you?"

"It's a form of attention."

"Punishing, isn't it? You can stop, today. Work on your golf swing. Go to Mexico for a few months. Adopt a baby."

"You're right. Being toxic poisons me." She laughed at her little joke. "Excuse me." She pulled out her cell phone and placed a call. "Matt. Can you get me on tomorrow? Exclusive. I want to tell everyone I've just been kidding."

I broke off a daffodil bloom and tucked it behind her ear. The soprano was joined by two others, and they harmonized like identical triplets.

ONLY A DAY left before I had to go back to school, not nearly enough time for all the people I wanted to influence. Bank of America's CEO. The chairman of Exxon Mobil. The NRA's president. All would have to wait. Heading home, intoxicated by my gift, I flew along the humming interstate.

"SHE'S MUCH BETTER," my mom said. "Straight As on her last report card."

Dr. Klein raised his caterpillar eyebrows.

"It's true," I said. "I'm running for student council president."

"Amazing."

"I'm promising an organic salad bar in the cafeteria. Of course, I have to shake a lot of hands." I decided not to tell him about my spring break trip. He was skeptical of my rapid improvement, and the miracles might seem unscientific.

He said the drug trial was ending and the blind would be broken.

"What do you mean?" my mom asked.

"We'll find out whether she's been taking the drug or a placebo."

I thought about this broken blind. If I found out the pills were nothing but sugar and filler, would the miracles cease? "Well, I don't want to know," I said. "Just give me a lifetime supply."

He chuckled. "Sorry, dear. It'll be at least a year before the FDA approves it."

I held up my bottle and rattle the lonely pill that was left. "What's it called?"

He leafed through a folder. "Um, looks like the name will be Chorus."

Wow. Suspicious, I asked about side effects.

"I don't know who's taking the drug versus the placebo. A couple of patients have reported constipation. Any problems like that?" He studied me over his glasses.

"No, no. What else?"

"One patient dropped out of the study. He had auditory and visual hallucinations. They went away when he quit taking the pills."

On the surface I was calm, reflecting Dr. Klein's twinkle right back at him. On the inside, my stomach had turned to concrete and my thoughts swirled in confusion. Aaron, my parents, Buddy Palleson, and Leigh Brackett—hadn't my touch simply freed

them to do the right thing? Made my fellow students notice me
and vote for my good ideas?

Or was I fooling myself?

After a sleepless night I knew what I must do. Google and the
Psylex website gave me a name: Dr. Garth Slate, Chief Scientist.
I swallowed the final pill, waited until he'd be home from
work then drove to his house, two towns over. He lived in an
immaculate Victorian, three stories high, pale gray with red and
black trim. All around it, flowers were a-bloom—tulips, violets,
and dandelion dots in the bright green lawn. A driveway curved
around to a garage, and there was Dr. Slate, a garbage bag in one
hand and an armful of newspapers in the other, walking towards
his trash bins. I was glad to see that he recycled.

My strategy was shaky. The drug—if that was what I'd been
taking and not a placebo—worked well. If Psylex didn't market
it, some other company would eventually come up with a similar
formulation. Well, he was the genius. He'd think of something.

Dr. Slate dropped newspapers into the blue bin. As he lifted
the garbage bag toward the gray bin, it split and spilled Slate
family trash all over the ground. "Fuck," he said.

I popped the trunk of Aaron's car, where he kept trash bags,
blankets, a first-aid kit, a flashlight, energy bars, and water, in
case he had a breakdown. I whipped out a couple of bags and
trotted down the driveway toward the mess. "Let me help you,
Dr. Slate!"

"Have we met?" He was a skinny guy, a fat-free runner. He
smelled like beer. "Are you a new neighbor?"

Why not? "Yes, I am. Let me give you a hand." I started
shoving crap into a bag. He tried to stop me but I pushed his
hand away. Sparkles filled the air and a woman's voice, a rich alto,
began to hum minor scales. "Got a scoop?"

He went into his garage and came out with a shovel. Together
we cleaned up the trash. "Nice of you," he said. "Neighborly."

I held out my hand and he had no choice but to take
it. The humming alto was joined by a mezzo counterpoint.
A glowing pink light flowed over us. "Can I have a glass of
water?" I asked.

Except for a vase of red tulips, the kitchen was hard and permanent: granite, stainless steel, marble. The oven gave off an herby chicken smell. He popped a Guinness, said his wife would be back soon, she'd gone to pick up their son. I refused the beer he offered but took a Pepsi. I didn't have much time and got right to the point.

"I'm in the Chorus drug trial and experiencing some unusual side effects."

"Lights, singing? Harmless. Hence the name."

"Has anyone mentioned a certain, um, ability?"

"Very rare. Why, you?"

"Definitely."

"You have a certain genetic variation that enhances your response to the drug." He took the lid off a pot and poked inside with a spoon.

"Please sit down, Dr. Slate. This is vitally important."

"Call me Garth." He turned a chair backwards and sat astride. "You know that Chorus works. The company needs a money-maker. We owe it to our shareholders."

"Your shareholders are mutual funds. You owe them nothing."

He looked glum and picked at his nails.

"Think back. Has Psylex ever *not* gone to market with a drug, after trials?" I asked.

"Of course. After the Vioxx scare, we stopped the development of our own COX-2 inhibitor. And there was a gout drug that also opened arteries. Looked good, until thromboses killed a few." He sipped his beer. "If the hazards outweigh the benefits, we stop development. In the case of Chorus, I can't define the hazards. Not in so many words. How can I say it . . . Delusional? Intensified grandiosity? Narcissistic?" He laughed. "Describes our board of directors. It doesn't seem like a big deal to me. What's your name, anyway?"

He didn't get it. I had to touch him, make him understand. I took my glass to the sink behind him, then twirled quickly and grabbed him around his middle. He sagged against me. A tenor voice began a smooth ooo-ooo-ooo and the air pulsated purplely. It was so beautiful that I got goose bumps.

"Chorus must never go to market," I told him, stroking his forehead. "It's prescribed for the mentally ill. It could go to someone who deciphers secret messages in the dictionary. Someone who's chewed through his leather straps. You cannot give a crazy person the power to manipulate people." I ran my finger along the rim of his ear, intensifying the tenor's flawless falsetto.

"Of course. There's too much potential for harm." He sighed. "I'll have to report some deaths. Is there a word for this? Falsifying results to keep a drug *off* the market?"

"It's ironic, Garth."

"Hey, thanks. For being my conscience." He slapped the floor, disturbing the glow, which shifted into the red spectrum. "Feels good. It's the right thing to do."

THAT NIGHT I dreamed about Mary Bee, her silky white-blonde hair and plump little mouth. I didn't know why we broke up—we'd been perfect together, and would be again. I needed just one more chance.

It was time. I pulled up in front of her house, strode to the front door, and rang the bell.

Mary Bee opened the door and I reached out and took her hand. Her precious face creased in a smile.

"I've missed you, Mary Bee." I didn't ask her for anything, at least not out loud. She knew.

"Same here." She pressed against me and I felt her heart beating. Her damp hair smelled like apples. I listened hard for a musical voice, but heard only the tinkle of a wind chime, a wren's shrill warble, a distant barking dog, the whisper of her breath as she kissed me with her salty-sweet, delicate mouth.

#grenadegranny

IT'S NOT DIFFICULT to rob a bank. The hard part is—cue drum roll—getting away with it.

How'd I get to this point in my life? I admit to a colorful past, but felonies weren't part of it. A few misdemeanors in my youth, a DUI last year, but overall Martha Sue Bly obeys the law. I even declare every penny of income from my laundromat, the Wishy Washy, to the IRS. You'll agree that's the very definition of honesty. Of course, since my quarters are deposited in the bank, which then reports them to the IRS, I don't have much choice.

Quite a racket, this coziness between banks and the US Government. When a bank can't pay what it owes, it's too big to fail and the US Government steps in with a bailout. When you or I run into financial misfortune, we get slapped with overdraft fees, repossession, foreclosure, and bankruptcy. Recently I was headed in that direction, with good reason to ponder the unfairness of this cozy relationship.

A few months ago I got a death sentence. Oh, not those words exactly. The doctor used terms like *rare, difficult to treat, aggressive. We can try this, Martha. Or that. No guarantees.*

It's not easy to obtain *this* or *that* when you've got no health insurance. Yup, I'm one of the unlucky North Carolina residents who earns too much for Medicaid, not enough for government subsidies. (Read that sentence twice. Because it doesn't make sense.)

I went through the Kübler-Ross stages in about three minutes flat: the lab musta made a mistake. But if they didn't—the doc's old, pushing sixty, so why not him instead? But since I got it—there's a chance, isn't there, with chemo and stem cells? Aw, there's no hope and I'm just gonna lie on the floor and cry for the rest of my short life.

It looked like forty-four years might be it for *moi*. What did I have to show for my too-short moment on this planet? A born-again evangelical daughter who said I was headed straight to hell to burn for eternity. A string of sorry men, evidence of a weakness for looks over brains, money, or character. Tattoos and cellulite.

Not very much. Somehow, that fact was even worse than my diagnosis.

THE WISHY WASHY is conveniently located in a strip mall right outside my neighborhood, Evergreen Hills, where the only hills are speed bumps and "green" is furnished by plentiful crabgrass, algae growing on our vinyl siding, and water in last summer's wading pools. The entrance is marked by a splintery sign that some hoodlum teenager took a mallet to, knocking off letters so that it now says v rg n Hills.

Three weeks into chemo, I pulled into my driveway with groceries and seven-hundred-dollars' worth of pills—thank you, AmEx. I was nauseated, tired, bald, and broke. My medical bills resembled a Wall Street bonus but the only hedge fund I knew of was my neighbor Robert's. Robert had come back from Afghanistan with a limp and a four-square-inch plate in his head. He was big as a fridge and good with tools, but simple. He earned money as a handyman—cutting grass, painting, spreading mulch, any little repair job you could think of. He lived at 312, next door to me, with his mom Annie, who used to be my best friend.

Robert was edging his sidewalk. "I almost didn't recognize you, Miss Martha," he said. "Where did your hair go?" Gotta love him.

"Don't know," I said. "It just fell out one day."

"You look real different. I never saw a bald lady before."

"There's a first time for everything. Your momma still working at the bakery?"

"Um, no. She was laid off. She's sleeping. Should I wake her up?"

"Let her sleep. I'll stop by later." A big fat lie. Annie and I weren't speaking. She claimed I stole her fiancé but if you ask me, I did her a favor. Smitty was lousy husband material. When

I got sick, he slithered away quicker than a bobcat onto his next prey—a dropout he found at the soft serve ice cream window. My feelings survived that blow, so should Annie's. I missed her, though, and most days I wished I had a friend like she used to be. I sighed and turned to get my grocery bags.

Robert laid the edger down. "Let me help you, Miss Martha."

"Bless you." I hadn't the strength of a newborn those days. He grabbed all five of my bags with one hand and jogged in front of me to get the door. "Lemonade?" I offered, once we were inside.

"Oh no, thank you, ma'am, I've got to get back to work. You need any help with your yard?"

My heart slipped in a sad direction as I pondered the boy. The man. He was about twenty-five, weighed over two-fifty, so tall he ducked going through doorways as a matter of habit.

I barely had enough for the phone bill but money was starting to look less and less important. "My beds sure do need weeding," I said. "And spread some mulch. I know you can make it look nice out front."

Too tired to put my groceries away, I lay down on the couch for a rest, until the phone rang. My spirits sagged when I saw it was Isabella with her dutiful-daughter weekly call. Is the average mom pleased to hear from her lovely daughter who lives in Charlotte in a million-dollar mansion with her perfect preacher husband and brilliant infant? Yes, of course she is.

Me, not so much.

"Hi, darling," I said, drumming up a bit of vocal enthusiasm.

"Mom, how are you?" Isabella meant, Are you sober? I hadn't told her about my health problems because she would imply they were divine retribution for my lifestyle.

"Good, I'm very good. How are you?" I braced myself.

"You got the package, right?"

Take a moment to imagine what a wealthy daughter might send to her cash-strapped mom. A fruit-and-cheese arrangement, perhaps, with a selection of fancy crackers and soups. A gift card for a dog groomer—my mutt's appropriately named Scruffy. Or what I really need: a note that says "please send me the roofer's bill once he's fixed that leak into your bedroom."

But Isabella's package had contained religious tracts. Flimsy paper booklets, the end of the world (coming soon!!!), the wages of sin, who gets into heaven and who doesn't. She's underlined passages and written in the margins: *it's never too late. So important. His love will save you.*

"Thank you," I said, gritting my teeth. "Very thoughtful."

"Jesus loves you, Mom, no matter what you've done."

She didn't know the half of what I've done. Perhaps Jesus did, though. "I'm glad to hear that, honey. Kiss the baby for me." And a prayer wouldn't hurt either. I hung up, sighed, and turned to Scruffy for some puppy love. Though shaggy bangs covered his dark expressive eyes, he managed to find my face for a sloppy kiss. Why did Issy's calls make me feel so lonely? My bones ached as my thoughts skittered from one regret to another.

Coulda been a better mom, not shuffled Issy off to her dad's to be indoctrinated by his holier-than-thou second wife.

Shoulda gone to college. Was having too much fun pouring drinks at Spanky's.

Woulda been happier (and wealthier) after my divorce if I hadn't married Trevor on the rebound. Trevor was smooth as glass, confident, and charming. How was I to know he made a living scamming snowbird seniors? Seasonal work. Each May he'd come back to North Carolina for six months. We were currently separated; neither of us could afford the price of a divorce.

Regrets, I had a few. I closed my eyes, tried to clear my brain, and dozed off until my doorbell rang.

"Come see, Miss Martha," Robert said. He'd trimmed the holly hedge, weeded the flower bed by my front steps, and even planted impatiens, red, pink, and white. With dark mulch, mine was the nicest house on the street. "I'll water these the next few days," he said. "No charge."

"Wonderful job, Robert." I paid him fifty dollars plus cost of the supplies. Mostly in quarters and ones, but he was happy, trotting home to show his mother.

I was putting my groceries away, slowly, when Annie knocked on my back door and walked right in, bearing a box. She's built like a fireplug, a look tempered by abundant black hair, dimpled chin, and a rosebud mouth currently set in a frown. Awash with joy at the sight of my friend, I wrapped my arms around her for a full minute. "I have no words," I breathed into her ear. "Missed you."

She took my face in her hands. "You didn't tell me you were getting chemo. And look at those cheekbones—you're not eating enough. Here, I made you some cupcakes."

I opened the box and gasped. "These are beautiful!" Each fat cupcake was perfectly swirled with frosting and decorated—blue with a white daisy, lime-green with chocolate hearts, lavender with silver sprinkles. Just seeing them lifted my spirits.

"Made with cannabis butter. I hear it helps with chemo. Don't tell Robert." She took over, efficiently sorting my groceries into fridge, pantry, fruit bowl.

"Oh my God, Annie, pot cupcakes. You are the best friend ever. And I'm sorry about Smitty."

"Not to worry. You did me a big favor, actually. Now taste one. I'm on a diet, can't even sample them. They're low dose but go easy." She creased each grocery bag and folded it into a rectangle.

It was hard to decide. "What's this one?" White frosting speckled with orange zest and shaved chocolate.

"Chocolate cake, orange-infused buttercream." Annie picked up a pencil and started wandering through my house, making notes. I wasn't too curious, being occupied with going easy. Meanwhile, the cannabis (which I couldn't taste) soothed my stomach, the chocolate and orange fired up my brain's pleasure centers, and this homemade gift eased my soul.

"Robert told me you were laid off," I said. "You could sell these online. Minus the pot."

"I've thought about it. Takes cash, honey. Licenses, website, supplies. We're barely existing on my unemployment." She shrugged, and her face looked worn. My moment of happiness faded as I realized how little I could do for Annie in return.

OVER THE NEXT few days neighbors dropped by. People I knew by sight, from brief chats at the Wishy, from patting their dogs when I was out with Scruffy.

Peter Jensen pushed his wife's wheelchair right up to my front steps. I'd never met her before. He'd always come to the Wishy by himself, towing a shopping cart of dirty laundry. He was a gentle quiet man. She was—well, neither.

"I'm Rosie," she said. "You've never met me because he can't hardly push me up the street in this thing." She pounded on the arms of her wheelchair. I murmured some pleasantry. "They sawed off my foot, you see?" She lifted the wool throw covering her legs, revealing a stump wrapped with stretchy bandages. "Diabetes. Couldn't afford the supplies, the food. But now it's the medical bills killing us, phew." She eyed me suspiciously, like I might be after her husband. Ha.

I wondered why they were here. To make me appreciate my feet?

"We brought you something," Peter said.

Rosie handed me a package wrapped in tissue paper. "I can't help or cook you nothing. But this I do."

I open the package. Inside, four knitted beanie hats, in pastel shades, variously trimmed with buttons, a tassel, ribbon. I blinked back a spurt of tears at her thoughtfulness. "Oh Rosie, thank you."

"I picked colors for your skin tone," she said. "You're a spring. Or were." Referring no doubt to my sickly hue and lack of locks. "Will be again."

DAWN SHOWED UP later. She was a fifty-ish woman who always talked with her hand covering her mouth because her teeth were blackened, crooked, or missing, like Rosie's foot. "Can't afford a dentist," she'd told me. She was renting a room from Peter and Rosie and looking for work. "But it's hard to get hired when you can't smile at people. Can't hardly let them see you talk." She asked to borrow Scruffy for an hour. He went willingly—he never met a stranger he didn't adore. She brought him back bathed and trimmed, with a jaunty red bow in his hair. This time I took deep breaths and didn't weep; I was getting used to kindness.

THE NEXT DAY I was at the Wishy, a no-longer-scruffy Scruffy at my feet and a pink tasseled hat warming my skull, when Annie came in and asked me for the key to my front door.

I held it up. "Why?"

"Just trust me."

"I don't want you going in my house. It's a mess." I'd been too exhausted to wash dishes, hang up clothes, or vacuum. Dog hair was second only to dust bunnies in square foot coverage.

"Relax." She took the key and left.

I settled down to counting my week's take, wondering what Annie wanted to do in my house. Maybe she was going to leave me another half-dozen pot cupcakes, bless her little baker's heart. I tried to think about what I could do for her in return, or for Rosie and Dawn. Maybe a Wishy Washy gift card.

I came home to a sparkling clean house. My clothes had been washed, ironed, and put away. Gone were the dog hair and dust bunnies. The kitchen counter, normally strewn with dirty dishes and unread mail, was scrubbed clean. Someone had even washed my windows and arranged a bouquet of tulips on the dining table. I knew those tulips—they came from Celina Robles' front yard. She and her husband José worked all hours selling fish tacos from their food truck. I called her to say thank you.

"Martha, you are very welcome. I hope you are not offended that I clean your house?"

Words failed me. Finally I managed to say, "Of course not. You didn't go out in your truck today?"

"Oh no, is broken. Something about engine rod throwing. So you see I have plenty of time and cleaning is easy for me. Look in your oven, we put some tamales."

Those damn tears. I choked out a "gracias" before checking the oven. Finding not only chicken tamales, but also some little tortilla things filled with apples and drizzled with Nutella. How did she know Nutella was my favorite condiment?

Oh, right. Annie. The woman was born to organize.

Lest I fail to mention—someone had fixed my roof too. I didn't know who.

THE NEXT MORNING I spent a half hour making up my sallow face into almost-pretty, getting ready for my weekly trip to the bank where I exchanged flirtatious innuendoes with the extremely hot teller Joshua, a thirty-something with manly stubble.

At the bank, I was filling out a deposit slip when a brouhaha broke out. Annie's son Robert wanted to cash a check he'd received from a client.

Joshua sounded apologetic. "Sorry, sir. We can't cash a third-party check for more than your account balance. Bank policy."

Robert was clenching his jaw, snorting through his nose, and working up to something he'd regret. I didn't blame him one bit—the raging unfairness of institutional coldness grabbed my attention. On impulse I reached around Robert and handed my bag of change and small bills to Joshua. "Put this in his account," I said.

Joshua looked startled, then at Robert for affirmation. The crazed look in Robert's eyes dimmed, was replaced by—tears? This six-foot man, tough as nails, tattooed with serpents and eagles and Semper Fi, rubbed his eyes. "Nicest thing . . . I'll pay you back next week," he mumbled.

It occurred to me he had probably fixed my roof; I'd seen him on top of his own house nailing down shingles. "No, no. Keep it," I said. Joshua started counting quarters, tension dissipated, Robert gave me a hug, like a cuddle from a grizzly. Need I say how good that felt? If I'd kept the money, it would've gone to pay my Visa bill, no happy feelings for anyone. But here I bought a smile and a hug with it. A new sensation, a bit of joy. When you don't have a future, what's money for?

That's when I decide to start robbing banks.

I DIDN'T INTEND to get caught. Not that I would've minded much—hello, free health care—but I had goals to meet first. I made a plan.

The bank had to be at least thirty miles from my house. It needed to have ample parking, a layout so I could make a quick getaway. The bank itself: not crowded—I didn't need witnesses or heroes who might interfere. A weekday morning to miss the lunch crowd, the closing rush.

The night before, I stole a license plate from a random car in a grocery store parking lot. How often do you check whether you still have a license plate? Never, right? The next morning, I screwed the stolen plate onto my beige Camry, the most common car in America. Every third car is a beige Camry.

I put on brown baggy pants and a baggier top, grabbed a small pillow for stuffing and a wig of short white curls. I'd bought an assortment of white wigs—chemo gave me an excuse. I slathered on an exfoliating facial mask that drew my skin into wrinkled cracks.

My target: a branch bank in a Winston-Salem shopping center. I parked in a quiet corner, tucked the pillow into my waistband, straightened my wig. Orange lipstick, a fake wart on my chin, sunglasses, moccasins and I was ready to rob and roll. Hunched over a little, walked kind slow. There's no one more invisible than a respectable granny.

Invisible, that is, until I reached the head of the line, showed the teller a metal pineapple, my pinkie tucked in the ring-pull, and handed her a note: *no bait, no dye pack. Just twenties, fifties, and hundreds, missy, all you got, spread 'em out where I can see 'em. Thank you very much and have a nice day.* ☺

The teller frowned. "Is this a joke?" she said.

"No, don't be rude." I waggled the grenade at her and she grew pale, got busy pulling bills out of her drawer.

"On the counter first," I said, "then slide them over here." I lowered my voice, spoke hoarsely.

She followed directions, I stuffed bills into a paper bag, and a minute later I walked out with over six thousand dollars. No one followed me as I got into my car and drove out of the lot, onto I-40 for the drive home. Trembling a little from thrill and adrenaline, I patted the bag. "I have plans for you," I said.

A video of my robbery was on the News at Ten. Exciting! The security camera had filmed a roundish elderly woman. Very wrinkled with a noticeable wart. My own daughter wouldn't have recognized me.

I washed off wrinkles and the wart, dusted my eyelids with smoky eyeshadow, and took the bills to my bank. I handed them to Joshua. "Will this buy me a night with you?"

"Martha, I would pay you." He winked. "I see you're laundering cash today."

"That's right. Give me half of that in a cashier's check." Neither of us mentioned that my deposit was four times the usual amount.

A FEW DAYS later, entering a bank for the second robbery, I looked entirely different. Black leather jacket, tweed skirt, black boots. White hair in a severe bob, lots of red lipstick and too much blush. Same grenade and note, however. Why change what worked? I escaped with four thousand plus change. Bought another cashier's check, deposited the rest, and went home to bed. The chemo still took its toll, though Annie's cupcakes helped with the worst symptoms.

FOR THE NEXT four banks I was variously a hippy with long white hair wearing a tie-dye caftan; an old lady lumberjack in one of Trevor's flannel shirts and red suspenders; stylishly unconventional senior in leopard-print leggings, a crocheted tunic, and braids; and punk granny, all in black, with a purple stripe in my white hair, showing cleavage and a dolphin tattoo.

A website went up with all my robbery videos and soon I even had my own hashtag. I'd never had so much fun. Not even when I was drinking. And the best came next.

I STARTED SPREADING the cash around, anonymously. After each robbery, one of my neighbors would make a pleasant discovery.

In his driveway, Robert found a gently used Ford van, painted shiny orange, with Robert's Handyman Services No Job Too Big or Small in green. On the front seat was a gift card to a home improvement store for $2000, for tools. I was walking Scruffy when he came out of his house. The look on his face was priceless.

A motorized wheelchair was delivered to Rosie's house. In a side pocket she found a cashier's check for $2000 with an anonymous note directing her and Peter to hire Robert to build them an entrance ramp and revamp their bathroom. I met her tooling down the street. As she bubbled about her new-found independence, I felt something new and tender inside. I didn't know a word for it. Like an ache was gone.

Dawn received a phone call from a dentist. Her dental implants were paid for; did she want to make an appointment? She was so excited when she told me. "As soon as I can smile, I'm going to call all the vets in town and offer my services as a dog groomer. Will you give me a reference?"

"You bet," I told her. "So will Scruffy."

José and Celina's mobile food truck disappeared. They didn't report it stolen—no insurance—which was just as well, because three days later it re-appeared, freshly painted, with a rebuilt engine, new tires and brakes, a new fryer. They parked their truck outside the Wishy, and I was the first customer, asking for three apple Nutella taquitos.

A package of business cards, brochures, boxes, and bags—all decorated with a charming logo for Annie's Cupcakery and containing the link to her new website—was delivered to Annie's door. A $4000 cashier's check for a computer, start-up supplies, and a social media consultant was icing on the cake, so to speak. I was visiting her when she opened it. It was so much fun to watch her go through the box, squeal at each little design detail. After a while she grew quiet and gave me an odd look. "A good fairy has moved to Oak Leaf Court," she said.

"I know! And I'd like to place the first order. A dozen assorted cupcakes. You know, the ones with the special ingredient." I shipped them to Issy, warning her not to let the baby have any.

SO MY GOALS had been achieved, I hadn't been caught, the chemo had bought me some time. My hair had grown back into sort of a curly pixie, and I'd gained weight, thanks to Nutella taquitos. My cheeks were rosy, my step was light. All was well—as well as possible, anyway—in Martha Sue Bly's world.

Until it wasn't.

THE FIRST OF May. Annie and I were in my kitchen taste-testing her latest creation, tiramisu cupcakes. "Someone's gotta do it," I joked as I inhaled vanilla bean cake with marscapone frosting, dusted with cocoa. We were having fun, exchanging stories about Smitty, our ex-in-common, when the front door opened and my almost-ex Trevor walked into my house. "Martha Sue, sweetheart!" he said. "Your hair is different. I like it."

Trevor makes an excellent impression with his dark floppy hair, broad shoulders, sapphire eyes. Annie sat up a little straighter and I heard her hum until I whispered, "He's a sociopath. Watch and learn."

I accosted my husband. "Uh, you heard of calling? Or even knocking?" I was feeling sassy. Joshua had asked me to run away with him when he took my deposit that morning.

"It's my house too, remember?" Trevor smiled at Annie. "Nice to meet you, darlin'."

"Not exactly. I make the payments."

"According to North Carolina law—" Here Trevor cleared his throat, his intro to all pompous pronouncements. I braced myself. "Half," he said, lowering his head and glaring at me. Just the one word, like I'd know what he meant. I felt cold all over as a stiletto of fear pierced me. Could he know about the robberies? How? All my fun vanished and I asked Annie to come back later because Trevor and I had to discuss some things in private.

She gave me a look—are you sure?—and when I nodded yes, she left.

Trevor wasted no time in stating his objective. "You owe me half of everything. Community property, right? I also want my red suspenders and blue flannel shirt back."

Oh no. I'd been so careful to disguise myself, then he'd recognized the lumberjack outfit I wore at bank #4. His clothes. Dummy! "I don't know what you're talking about."

"Of course you do, Grenade Granny."

He was right. Though blackmail was a felony, so was robbing banks. "I've given the money away to my neighbors. They've helped me out because I've been sick." I didn't want tell him the details of my illness. Trevor's attempts at fake sympathy would nauseate me.

"Then you need to hit one again, don't you? Make enough to give me my share?"

I sighed, feeling lower than the day I got my diagnosis. "I guess so. Give me a couple of weeks."

"I'll be on your doorstep in two days. Twenty thousand in cash is perfectly acceptable."

SO I GEARED up for one last haul. This time I donned a white pageboy wig, black wrap dress, padded bra, high heels, and sunglasses. I was hardly invisible granny but the hair covered much of my face, the glasses hid my eyes, and I added some fake teeth to give me an overbite. I could see the headlines . . . Grenade Granny Goes Glam. The trembling teller gave me nine thousand dollars, the biggest haul yet.

On my way out of the parking lot, I pulled off the wig and removed the teeth, then stopped at a fast food restaurant to strip off my dress and bra and slip into shorts and sandals. All the bank's money went into an envelope for Trevor.

In a cloud of anxiety I walked up to the Wishy and collected the bills from the change machine, quarters from the washers and dryers. The place was busy, but no one from Oak Leaf Court was there. Maybe they'd all bought washers and dryers with their newfound prosperity. I was frantic with worry over Trevor. Paying him blackmail money might just whet his appetite for more. And if I balked and he told the police I was Grenade Granny, they might figure out where the money had gone. Scandal would rain down on Oak Leaf Court. I had nowhere to turn.

I dabbed on mascara and a red lippy and went to the bank with my regular deposit. My unhappiness must have showed on my face, because Joshua frowned. "Say it's not true," he said, counting my money. "That you've found someone else and you're dumping me. " His hazel eyes studied me.

I made an effort. "There will never be anyone else. You smell too good, like pine and lemon and the sea."

"Then what's wrong?"

"Nothing, I'm fine." I forced a smile but he didn't return it. He handed me the deposit slip, on which he'd drawn a pair of hearts linked by an arrow.

For the first time in a year, I felt desperate for a drink. But alcohol wouldn't have cured my ills, only created more problems. I went home and waited for Trevor to arrive on my doorstep.

HE NEVER CAME.

Trevor had been murdered. His body was found that night, underneath the stadium seating at a Greensboro high school. He'd been stabbed four times in the back. Estimated time of death, late morning, so I had an alibi—I'd been seen in the Wishy and at the bank. Not that I was a suspect—why should I be?

His other wife wasn't a suspect either. Yes, it turned out that Trevor was a bigamist with a wife in Florida, which partly explained his six-month absences. She and I commiserated over our similar miserable Trevor-experiences.

Detectives found a few of his scamming victims and questioned them, but finally concluded it must have been a mugging, since Trevor's wallet and phone were missing.

I didn't believe it was a mugging, or a scamming victim. I suspected who killed Trevor. And I was grateful.

A WEEK LATER, on the Riviera Maya. Joshua and I reclined in a private cabana, avoiding the heat of the day, drinking pisco sours. Mine was virgin, but nonetheless tasty. Also tasty was Joshua, who turned out to be even sexier once he emerged from the bank. I'd shown him the ad for this resort as a joke but he thought I was serious, and maybe I was. And here we were, me and my boy-toy.

"Pour me another, please," I said. "All those quips about money laundering. How did you know?"

"I'll tell you but you won't like it." He handed me the drink and rested his hand on my thigh. His hand was warm and brown and very capable. "I recognized you in the first video."

"What? I was invisible granny with a wart!"

"You looked right at the camera at one point. I saw your eyes. These eyes." He leaned over and kissed my closed eyes, left, right. "I didn't know why, but I remembered when you gave Robert your money, and I thought . . . you were a woman on a mission."

I inhaled his smell, pine and the sea. "Why didn't you turn me in?"

"Guess I liked your mission. Spread happiness."

"Until Trevor showed up, it was working." I told him about Trevor's murder. "Someone saved me."

"Who?"

I remembered how Annie left my house the day Trevor threatened to blackmail me. Did she go home? Or lurk under my kitchen window to listen to us talk? I thought about Annie's amazing organizational skills on my behalf, getting my good neighbors to clean my house, fix my roof, knit me pretty caps, groom Scruffy, cook delicious foods that I could eat, thanks to her pot cupcakes. I thought about the morning Trevor was killed, how none of those neighbors were in the Wishy Washy. What else, who else, had Annie organized?

"It doesn't matter," I said. "Let's go for a swim." I took his hand in mine and we walked across the white sand, into a sparkling turquoise sea.

Blessings

SURELY IT'S DISCRIMINATION to deny a job to a woman who earned her cosmetology license in prison. Especially when she has been *exonerated*. Declared *innocent*. But it seems no one will take a chance on me. After the umpteenth salon manager asks where I've worked, responds thanks-but-no-openings, and hangs up, I decide to try a personal approach, make use of my beauty-pageant glow. What's left of it, after seven years in lockup.

There's a strip mall across the highway from my apartment. Grocery store, dry cleaners, pizza joint, and a hairdresser's called Park Avenue. A hoity-toity name for a low-rent joint. Walk-ins welcome. I peer through a smudged window. Stuffing's popped out of the sofa cushions and the floor tiles—a few missing—are grimy. The walls are what some call apple green—but I think, yeah, maybe after the apple's been digested.

A spiky-haired teenager lies on the ripped sofa thumbing her phone. She's pierced every which way to Sunday. The piercings don't spoil her natural beauty because she hasn't got any. She hollers, "Mom! You got a customer!"

Mom emerges, wearing a blond Dolly Parton wig and a pink strapless terry sundress one size too small. (I can't abide wearing strapless when you're doing hair. I like a bit of fabric between armpit and customer.) She stares at me. I get that a lot, being six-one. Her mouth's open but nothing comes out except a foul cigarette odor.

I hold out my hand for a shake and say that I'd be so pleased to talk with her about renting a space in her salon. I amp up my glow—thanks to Mama's lessons in superficial charm—and compliment her on her place, failing to mention the hairy dust bunnies and overflowing waste bins. She nods but I can't tell what she's thinking. She asks my name and I hesitate a second—too many people have heard of Brea Casteel. But she doesn't blink, says her name is Polly Park.

Polly leads me through the deserted salon to a cubicle in the back. Scummy basin, stained counter, chair covered with splattered dye. My heart sinks, I'm tired of dirty places. On the plus side, there's a window (with a view of dumpsters) and Polly says I can do the space up any way I like. She tells me that two other stylists work there, part-time afternoons, and the rent's one-fifty. There's no receptionist—everyone books their own clients, furnishes their own supplies. I wait for it but she doesn't ask where I trained or where I've worked.

"What do you think, Brea? Ready to join the Park Avenue team?" Polly sounds unsure and I realize she's as insecure about her crummy salon as I am about my entire life. Somehow that makes me feel better about the place. Room for improvement wherever you look.

Feeling brave, I sign a six-month lease and write her a check. She gives me a key, shows me the bathroom, ugh, and a break area, more ugh, cluttered with trash and diet soda cans and dirty dishes. I glance at Polly—she's OK with the mess? She's already turned her back to tell her texting daughter, get ready to leave. I'm thinking this place would not be acceptable to Mama. Even when we lived in our car she kept it clean and organized.

"You can have mornings," Polly says. "You'll be alone then, you'll catch all the walk-ins. Start tomorrow?"

Two stylists have wandered in. One ignores me. She's about twenty-five, with pink-streaked black hair, too much eyeliner and a sullen expression like one of the undead. The other is a brick-shaped woman with bright red lipstick, but she's friendly, welcoming me with a quick smile. Polly tells me their names are Eve (the undead) and Dru (red lipstick). I feel a little shy, like it's the first day in a new school. I spent fifteen years faking it in beauty competitions, a year as a nanny while I slept with the husband until I was convicted of murdering the wife, then seven years surrounded by felons. It's no surprise that I don't quite know how to act around civilians. Will they see through my too-tall exterior to the freak, despite my efforts to glow? In prison, we were so sad, all wanting the same things—keys, a job, a warm being in the night. Friendship was a hollow substitute.

AT NINE THE next morning, I insert my key into Park Avenue's front door (loving my keys, loving how they unlock doors). I want to catch any walk-ins since I'm broke, my cash tied up in supplies.

The hours pass slow as jail time. I sweep the floor, polish my mirror, clean the plate glass window though spatters of rain tell me no sane woman would get her hair done in this weather. I paint my nails midnight blue. I make coffee. A cloud of worry, the fear of poverty ingrained in my DNA, drifts around me and nothing will scatter it but clients, a steady stream of them, one every hour, every day.

I'm thinking about a plant for my counter—maintenance-free ivy, sexy orchid, or soft fern?—when—hallelujah—a man walks into Park Avenue. He's fifty-ish, balding on top but long on the sides and back. Not a good look, but he wants it all off. After a #1 buzz cut, I tell him he resembles Patrick Stewart. Throughout he doesn't say a word, doesn't give me a tip even though I've worked my glow for all it was worth. Maybe he hates that I'm taller than he is, I think, pocketing eighteen dollars and starting another coat of nail polish. He goes to the door then comes back, hands me a five. "Sorry, I was rude. Lots on my mind today."

I'm curious. In my experience, people rarely apologize. Every jerk thinks he's justified.

"My assistant has quit, I've got an event today that I can't cancel and I badly need help. Could you give me a hand? Two hours, fifty bucks?"

I sweep my hand at the empty salon. "What, and leave all this?"

He runs his hand around the back of his head. "Harrigan's. It's just down the road. What do you say?"

The job would fill some time, and I need the money. "Sure. As soon as someone else takes over here."

"See you later, then." He bustles out the door, leaving me slightly more optimistic about my future.

Dru, her lipstick even brighter than yesterday's, drags in around noon. I tell her about my gig down the road. "A place called Harrigan's, you know it?" It sounds like the name of a pub.

She shudders. "That's a funeral home! As in, dead people. Creeps me out. You gonna do hair?"

Oh. Well, even dead people want to look good. Er, deserve to look good.

THE RAIN HAS stopped, and steam rises from the hot pavement as I walk a quarter-mile to Harrigan's Funeral Home, an enormous Victorian with porches, turrets, oodles of gingerbread. Inside, dim light, flowered carpets, sofas like big bricks, a fireplace.

"Call me Tim." He gives me a quick tour of the casket showroom, pointing out options. Satin or velvet? Maple, mahogany, oak, or pine? Handles, trim, pillows. More than I ever thought I'd know about caskets. Mama died while I was in prison and her body was cremated. I don't even know what happened to her ashes. I listen politely to Tim, wondering what he needs me to do. Finally, after a brief walk through the chapel, past massive buckets of pungent lilies (for some reason, lilies smell like hot dogs to me), he gets to the point. Showing me a program for a viewing, he says I have to get Mrs. Jolly ready.

"Hair and makeup. And help me dress her. You'll see. It takes two." He's matter-of-fact, though he's watching me for a reaction.

"No worries." Indeed, I feel prepared for anything. He leads me to the back of the building, into a well-lit room with a concrete floor, sinks, hoses, steel instruments. On a table rests a body, covered up to the neck by a sheet. Mrs. Jolly's plump face is a healthy pink color. Her hair, dyed reddish-brown with an inch of white roots, hangs over the end of the table at least a foot.

"She's already been embalmed," he says.

I nod, glad I don't have to participate in that. "What hairstyle, do you think?"

Tim shrugs. "I didn't get a picture from the family. Use your judgment. All we care about is the front and sides." He shows me a cabinet with supplies.

We wheel the table to a sink where I give Mrs. Jolly her final shampoo and blow-dry. I spray root concealer on her white stripe, and brush it in. Tim helps me prop her up a bit so I can scissor her bangs, fluff them up and trim the hair all around. We lay her back and I finish with the blow-dryer and a spritz of hair spray. I powder her face, add brown eye shadow and black mascara to her eyes, which are mostly closed, just a sliver of cloudy eye visible. After blush and a touch of coral lip gloss, except for her eyes she looks alive, like she might jump up, dance, and sing. I dab pearly polish on Mrs. Jolly's nails. Her hands are hard, like plastic.

"She looks younger," Tim says, "very nice. Let's get her dressed." He brings out a cocktail dress, a teal-blue chiffon.

"What about shoes?" If the shoes are open-toed, I should paint her toenails.

"The casket will be only half open. Besides, look." He lifts the sheet.

Mrs. Jolly has no feet. They are missing, removed at the ankle. Her legs end in squared-off stumps.

My self-control evaporates like breath on a mirror, and I gasp for air. I had thought I was fine, feelings successfully squelched. But Mrs. Jolly's clammy plastic skin, sweet-rotten smell, slivers of dead eye, and the final straw—missing feet—combine with the utter freakishness of this place to press down on me and I give way. I feel a whirring sensation in my head, the floor tilts up, and the world vanishes.

When I awake, apparently only a few seconds later, Tim has put a pillow under my head. He holds out a cup of water. "It takes a while to get used to. You're not the first to pass out and you won't be the last."

"What happened to her feet?" I push myself to a sitting position, embarrassed, breathing slowly.

"Wasn't what killed her. That happened a long time ago, from the looks of them. You OK? Go outside for a minute, get some air." He points to a hall, a back door. "Hope you'll come back, though. I need your help to dress her."

The air is fresh after rain, humid and clean. I sit on the steps, remove my shoes, and rub my feet on damp grass. A bunion is beginning on my left foot, my little toes curl under. I circle my feet clockwise, then counter-clockwise. Flex my ankles, point and wiggle my toes.

What would it feel like to have no feet? Legs that stop at the ankle? My mind clamps shut, refusing to entertain the idea. Don't go there, that's the way I got through the years in prison, refusing to look at certain things. How Cy betrayed me, how Angela lied, said I killed Fran. I rarely allowed myself to think those thoughts, turned my mind away from an empty present, a hopeless future. Denial is a skill, not showy like backflips or lucrative like safe-cracking, but useful.

I sip the water. Feet or no feet, Mrs. Jolly deserves to look good. Today's an important day for her. I slip my shoes on and hurry inside to help Tim wrestle her into the teal chiffon dress, maneuver her body into a velvet-lined mahogany casket with gold handles, and wheel her to her place of honor.

When Tim hands me fifty bucks, I apologize again for passing out.

"You were a big help." He has an open, likeable face. "Hope to call on you again." His round smooth head comes up to my chin.

AT PARK AVENUE, Dru is shampooing an actual client who's chattering away about a televised trial of a woman accused of killing her child, a program I surely will never watch, having had enough of courtrooms to last me to eternity and beyond.

Eve's in the break room touching up her eyeliner. I greet her with a cheerful "hi" but she shoots me a dark look, doesn't respond. Ah, feels familiar. Prison was full of women like her, lacking the energy for civility. She will warm up, I hope. Her skin is milky white, no visible pores, perfect.

I slump into my chair, struck by heart-thumping limbs-tingling stomach-clenching panic. I have committed myself to making a living in this dump, with no clients, no phone. I stare through the dusty window at the dumpsters, feeling sorry for myself, sorry for Mrs. Jolly's life without her feet, missing Mama. Then I hear her voice. *Brea Casteel, get your lazy ass up outa that chair, and count your blessings. Do what needs to be done, little missy.* Even towering over her by a good ten inches I was always *little missy.*

Tears fill my eyes—I miss her so much—and I slip into the bathroom for a two-minute cry, wishing she was beside me, thinking how I always depended on her pushing me. *Count your blessings*, she said. I count. My own apartment with a bathtub and a key. Thinking back on Mama's last months, I remember it's a blessing to be healthy. I grab a piece of paper and start writing it all down in case I need reminders. Real coffee, butter pecan ice cream in the freezer, giant pine trees that creak in the wind. My feet, ha. A place to do hair though it needs cleaning. *Do what needs to be done, little missy.*

I find a sponge, Pine Sol, and a bucket. I wash my window, inside and out. I scrub every surface of my station—sink, counter, chair, floor. Dru comes back to my cubicle. "You're a hard worker."

I'm on the floor, giving it a final wipe. "It's still drab."

"The green's pukey. None of us like it."

"What about a different color? Would Polly mind?"

"She don't care. Might even cheer her up. She's getting chemo, you know."

That explains the wig, and more. Mama lost interest in her surroundings when she got sick, too. "I'll have to ask her permission," I say.

Dru looks around at the dispirited dump that is Park Avenue and snorts. She calls out to Eve. "Brea wants to paint the place. What color, you think?"

Eve looks up from her magazine. "Purple. Smoky purple."

"I like it," Dru says.

"I don't have a car," I say, "but I'll buy the paint."

Eve waves her hand dismissively. "We'll all chip in. Let's surprise Polly and do it tonight."

"Mirror tiles are cheap," I say, remembering how Mama put them up for a kitchen backsplash in our double-wide. "We can stick them on our counters."

AROUND SIX WE start to work, painting the salon's walls a color called Purple Haze, the trim a pale gray. We cover the floor with marbled gray peel-and-stick floor tiles, an impulse buy after Dru spotted four boxes on the fifty-percent-off table.

We work like women possessed, mostly quiet until Eve starts with the dirty jokes. She's practicing for open mike at a club called The Joke Joint, and I laugh and gasp until my face hurts though I wonder why, Eve, with your sweet deadpan face and milky skin, are you spewing shocking stories, filthy language? Dru and I agree she'll be a real hit and we'll be there to cheer her on.

The ripped sofa will go to the dump, to be replaced by these armless leather chairs Dru had spotted in the Habitat store.

"Brandi won't have anywhere to lie down," I say. Polly's texting daughter had owned the couch yesterday.

"Brandi can take her decorative self to the break room. Anyway, she and Polly won't be here for a few days. Polly's going in for another treatment tomorrow." Dru looks at her watch. "Oops. It's after midnight. Guess I mean today."

I have a little surprise for them. On each of our counters I place three tea lights. They flicker against the mirror tiles.

"Ooo, pretty," Dru says. Under specks of Purple Haze, her face shines with fatigue.

Eve smiles, showing a mouthful of braces, transforming herself from undead into pretty. "We're glad you've joined us, Brea," she says, and I'm overcome with the oddest sensation. I can't name it, it's new and tender. I hold my breath, cherishing the way I feel.

Karen Pullen's restless dreams were achieved when she escaped the cubicle and took up fiction writing. After earning an MFA from Stonecoast at the University of Southern Maine, she published two traditional mystery novels, *Cold Feet* and *Cold Heart*, both with Five Star Cengage, and numerous short stories. Karen serves on the national board of Sisters in Crime, and works as an innkeeper, editor, and teacher of writing. She lives in Pittsboro, North Carolina, and blogs occasionally on her website, karenpullen.com.

Printed in the USA
CPSIA information can be obtained
at www.ICGtesting.com
LVHW052148180923
758603LV00005B/71